BEAGLE IN A BASKET

'Hi there, Robbie,' Mandy said cheerfully, giving the beagle a pat. 'Hey, what's the matter? You don't look very happy.'

'He isn't, I'm afraid,' said Geraldine with a wan smile. 'I'm really worried about him.'

'Well, I suppose he's bound to be upset for a while,' Mandy replied. 'He'll be missing Martha, won't he?'

'No, you don't understand,' said Geraldine, her voice rising as she became more agitated. 'He doesn't want to go outside, and he won't eat, either. And you know how he normally loves his food. I think there's something seriously wrong with Robbie!'

Animal Ark series

Plus:

LUCY DANIELS

Beagle
— in a —
Basket

Illustrations by Ann Baum

*Hodder
Children's
Books*

a division of Hodder Headline Limited

To Vivien Hylton of Byleeton Beagles –
thank you for my own special beagle, Bob

Special thanks to Jennie Walters

Thanks also to C.J. Hall, B.Vet.Med., M.R.C.V.S., for reviewing
the veterinary information contained in this book.

For more information about Animal Ark,
please contact www.animalark.co.uk

10 9 8 7 6 5 4 3 2 1

A Catalogue record for this book is available from the British Library

ISBN 0 340 85111 2

Typeset by Avocet Typeset, Brill, Aylesbury, Bucks

Printed and bound in Great Britain by Clays Ltd,
Bungay, Suffolk

Hodder Children's Books
a division of Hodder Headline Limited
338 Euston Road
London NW1 3BH

One

'Excuse me, love! This is the vets' place, isn't it?'

Mandy Hope looked up from the bicycle tyre she had just finished pumping. A large man with a flushed, shiny face was calling to her from the open window of his sports car. 'That's right – Animal Ark,' she replied, pointing up at the carved wooden sign swinging gently in the breeze. 'But we're not really open yet – unless it's an emergency, of course.'

'Well, the thing is, I can't hang around,' the man said anxiously, mopping his forehead with a large spotted handkerchief. 'I've had a terrible time catching this little fellow, and I'm going to be late for my first appointment. You couldn't help me get him out of the car, could you?'

With a great deal of effort, the man levered himself out of the driver's seat. Mandy couldn't help wondering how such a big person could possibly be comfortable in such a small car.

'Lovely set of wheels, isn't she?' the man went on proudly, following Mandy's gaze and patting the car's gleaming bonnet. 'Goes like a rocket. I've had her for fifteen years, you know – since I was a young slip of a lad. Can't bear to part with her.'

That explains it, Mandy thought to herself, trying not to smile. *You're certainly not a slip of a lad now.* 'So what have you brought us?' she asked, leaning her bike against the wall and peering into the car. She was curious to see exactly what kind of creature he'd managed to catch.

'Well, I spotted the poor thing in a ditch by the side of the road,' the man replied, not exactly answering her question. 'His leg seems to be hurt pretty badly. I managed to scoop him up and put him in an old box in the car, but he found a way out of it. Now he's gone under the passenger seat and I can't get at him.' He paused and looked at Mandy. 'I'm Geoff Bates, by the way, sales rep for sweets and chocolates. Must have driven past your sign a hundred times on my rounds. Never thought I'd stop off one day!'

He walked round to open the passenger door and raised his eyebrows at her. 'Reckon you're just about the right size to reach the little fellow,' he said. 'Could you give it a go?'

'Well, I'll do my best,' Mandy replied, going round to join the man at the other side of the car. There was no way she could hear about a sick or injured creature without wanting to lend a hand. Tucking her blonde hair behind one ear, she crouched down to take a cautious look under the passenger seat. Wounded animals were often frightened and could lash out suddenly, so she was ready to retreat if necessary.

A pair of beady round eyes stared back at her, set in a glossy green head. A male mallard duck was nestling in a shadowy cave under the leather passenger seat. The floor was littered with crumpled chocolate-bar wrappers, and he seemed to have made himself quite comfortable among them. He didn't look like he was going anywhere in a hurry.

'Can you see him?' Mr Bates asked, from somewhere behind her. 'What's he up to?'

'He's just sitting there. He looks happy enough, though,' she reported, and she heard the man groan.

'I won't be in York till ten at this rate,' he muttered.

Mandy sat back on her heels and wondered what to do. She could just about reach the duck, but if she backed him into a corner he might become aggressive. That strong beak of his could strike a nasty blow, and she wasn't wearing gloves. Suddenly, she had a brainwave.

'Can you reach in from the other side and make a noise behind the seats?' she asked, turning round to look at Mr Bates. 'I think that way we might be able to flush him out. I'll be ready to catch him here.'

'Good idea!' he replied promptly, and he hurried round to open the door on the driver's side. Mandy took off her school jumper and held it ready to throw over the duck when he emerged.

'Out you come, little duckie,' called Mr Bates in a high voice, making a scrabbling sound on the back of the passenger seat with his fingers. His large bottom was up in the air as he leaned head first into the car, and his face was turning redder and redder with effort. Mandy had a terrible feeling she was going to burst out laughing, so she tried not to look at him. *Don't be mean*, she told herself sternly. *At least he took the trouble to stop and help – lots of people would have just driven past.* She forced herself to concentrate on what they were trying to do.

The duck gave a low, hoarse call and Mandy prepared herself as she willed the bird to come out. She watched intently as Mr Bates called and thumped more loudly on the back of the seat, beginning to lose patience. And then, with a very indignant quack, the tip of a yellow beak emerged and the mallard struggled out into the open, dragging one webbed foot awkwardly behind him.

As carefully as she could, Mandy dropped her jumper on to his body and picked him up – holding him gently but firmly with his hurt leg facing away from her. 'It's all right,' she said comfortingly, feeling the frantic beating of his heart through her fingers. 'No one's going to hurt you.'

Carefully, she pulled her jumper free of the duck's head, so he could see where he was and she could take a closer look at him. The beautiful colours of his plumage shone in the sun. Below his gleaming green head, a sparkling collar of white feathers ringed his neck. His breast was a subtle purple, and soft grey feathers covered the underside of his body, contrasting with his dark tail. Mandy couldn't tell exactly what was wrong with the injured leg, but it looked swollen, and one broad, paddle-shaped foot hung uselessly. His eyes were dull, too. And then she spotted a telltale piece of nylon thread trailing from his leg.

'He's got caught up in some fishing-line, poor

thing,' she told Geoff Bates, who'd straightened up in relief and was wiping his face again with the spotted handkerchief. 'Can you help me take him inside? We'll need to get it off as quickly as possible. I think the surgery door's locked, but we can get there through the house.'

'Of course, of course,' Mr Bates replied, opening the gate for her and hurrying ahead down the path. 'I'm so grateful to you for helping me. I'd never have got him out on my own.' He lifted the latch and pushed open the front door, then stood back to let Mandy through.

The Hopes lived in an old stone cottage in the little Yorkshire village of Welford. The vets' surgery was in a modern extension at the back of the house, which Mandy thought was a perfect arrangement. It meant she could keep a close eye on any animals who had to stay in the residential unit for a few days, and she was often able to help out in the surgery too. Her parents, Emily and Adam Hope, were both vets, so animals had been an important part of her life for as long as she could remember.

The duck gave another harsh call of alarm and began to struggle in Mandy's hands as she carried him into the cottage. 'It's all right,' she said soothingly. 'We're just going to sort out that leg of yours.' Her father had gone out to a nearby farm early that morning but she knew her mother was at home, ready to start morning surgery.

'What's all this?' asked Mrs Hope, coming out of the kitchen. Her eyes widened in surprise as she saw Mandy holding the duck, with the large figure of Mr Bates hovering behind her.

'I found this drake by the side of the road,' he told Mandy's mum, almost apologetically. 'I couldn't think what else to do with him so I brought him here.'

'He's got some fishing-line wound round his

leg,' Mandy put in. 'Can you see the end of it there?'

'Oh, yes. Well spotted,' said her mother, holding back her long auburn hair as she bent forward cautiously to take a closer look at the mallard. He watched her warily from the safety of Mandy's arms. 'Looks like he's rather dehydrated, too,' Mrs Hope added, carefully prising open the duck's beak. 'Yes, his mouth is very dry inside. Never mind, I'm sure we'll be able to sort him out.'

'I can't pay a huge amount for his treatment,' Mr Bates said awkwardly, taking a small white card out of his pocket, 'but perhaps you could let me know what it's likely to cost. Here's my address and phone number.'

'Don't worry,' Mrs Hope said reassuringly, taking the card from him. 'I'm sure it won't come to very much.' Mandy caught her mother's eye and smiled. Emily Hope might be more businesslike than her husband, but she could still be a softie sometimes. Mandy felt sure that Mr Bates wouldn't be charged anything at all for his kindness.

'Marvellous!' he said, with a look of great relief. 'And now I really have to go, or I'll lose my job.' He rifled through the other jacket pocket and came up with a couple of chocolate bars. Putting them on a side table, he winked at Mandy and said,

'These are for later, since you've got your hands full now. Thanks for everything!'

As Mr Bates left, the duck began to strain against Mandy's grip again. 'Shall I take him straight through to the surgery for you, Mum?' she asked. 'I think he's getting a bit agitated.'

'No, thank you very much,' Mrs Hope replied firmly, shutting the front door behind Mr Bates and scooping the bird expertly out of Mandy's arms. 'Unless you hurry, you're going to be late for school as it is. Simon's opening up the surgery just now and I'm sure we can manage one little duck between us.' Simon was the practice nurse who helped the Hopes run Animal Ark, along with Jean Knox, their receptionist.

'But, Mum. . . !' Mandy protested. 'Can't I stay and help you?'

'School! Now!' replied Mrs Hope over her shoulder, already on her way through to the surgery extension. 'Don't worry, I'm sure he'll still be here when you get back.'

Mandy pedalled frantically along the road towards school. She usually cycled in with her best friend James Hunter, who also lived in Welford, but there was no sign of James this morning. He must have thought she'd gone in earlier and decided not to

wait for her. Mandy took one hand off the handle-
bar to snatch a quick look at her watch. She'd
already missed registration and she was going to
be late for the first lesson. It was Friday, so that
would be – oh, no, biology! She groaned, and
urged her aching legs to pedal faster. Biology used
to be her favourite subject, but it definitely wasn't
at the moment. Their teacher, Miss Temple, was
recovering from an eye operation and wouldn't be
back until after half-term. A supply teacher called
Mr Marsh was taking her classes while she was
away.

It was a couple of weeks into the summer term
now and, so far, Mr Marsh and Mandy weren't getting on very well. The trouble was, she found it very
difficult to concentrate during his lessons. Biology
was full of interesting information about plants
and animals, and her mind was always shooting off
at a tangent. Some fact Mr Marsh was explaining
might remind her of a patient back at Animal Ark,
for example, or a conversation she'd had with her
parents. But she soon discovered that their new
teacher hated being interrupted – unlike Miss
Temple, who always enjoyed a lively discussion.

'Yes, that's all very interesting, Amanda,' Mr
Marsh had said to her a couple of days before,
when she couldn't resist telling him how danger-

ous chocolate was for small animals like hamsters. 'However, I must remind you that we are talking about digestion in *humans*. And now can we please get back to the subject?'

As soon as she got to school, Mandy hastily flung her bike against the railings and dashed over to the biology lab. 'Sorry I'm late, Mr Marsh,' she said breathlessly, as she slipped into the classroom and took a seat by the front, trying not to make any noise.

'Just take your book out quickly,' he replied in an irritated voice, 'and write down this assignment. As I was telling the others, we'll be doing something different over the next couple of weeks. I want each of you to work on your own project. You can choose the subject, as long as it has something to do with the topics we've covered so far. And I want to see lots of research and scientific information, please – not waffle. This task is to help you organise your work, which *some* of you. . .' and here he glared at Mandy, who felt herself blush, '. . . need to do. You can work on your projects at home as well as in class, and I want you to make a start for homework this weekend. Please choose a topic and write a short outline plan, ready to hand in on Monday. Now, any questions?'

As the lesson continued, Mandy tried to concentrate on the complicated diagrams Mr Marsh was drawing on the board – but her mind was already racing. There were so many subjects she was interested in, she didn't know which one to choose. Perhaps she could write about how animals adapt to their surroundings. There was plenty she could find to say about that. Or maybe she would concentrate on animal travellers: birds who fly south in winter, or salmon who come back to the river in which they were born to lay their eggs. She was so busy thinking, she found it difficult to keep her mind on what Mr Marsh was saying, and once or twice he caught her looking out of the window. At the end of the lesson, he called her over.

'I think you and I need to have a chat, Amanda,' he began, loosening his tie and rubbing his neck. He was quite young – about the same age as Miss Temple, Mandy guessed – but he always wore a formal jacket and tie. Miss Temple was much more casual, with her flowery cotton dresses and wavy brown hair that never managed to stay neatly tied in a ponytail. She loved her subject, though. Mandy sighed, wishing Miss Temple was setting this assignment. They could have chosen a really interesting topic together.

She suddenly realised that Mr Marsh had

stopped talking, and was fixing his hazel eyes on her. 'You see?' he said in exasperation. 'You haven't been listening to a word I've been saying, have you? *And* you missed the beginning of the lesson this morning. It's just not good enough!'

'I'm sorry, sir,' Mandy replied, staring hard at her fingernails. She tried to explain. 'You see, I was late because—'

Mr Marsh held up one hand. 'No, I don't want to hear any excuses!' he said, shaking his head. 'Whatever happens at home, you must get to school on time. And when you *do* get here, you have to put everything else out of your mind and concentrate on what you are being taught. Is that quite clear, Amanda?'

'Yes, sir,' Mandy said, her cheeks burning again. She felt angry and confused. It was so unfair! There were lots of others in the class who didn't work nearly as hard as she did. Why was Mr Marsh picking on her?

Two

'Oh, come on, Mandy! Give it a rest,' James said, buckling on his helmet. 'It's the weekend now. No more Mr Marsh for two days.'

'I suppose you're right,' Mandy admitted, adjusting her schoolbag before pushing off. Having a good moan to James had already made her feel better and, besides, there was always plenty going on at Animal Ark to take her mind off things. 'Can you come home with me?' she called to him. 'There's a new patient you have to meet!'

By the time they'd arrived back in Welford, her bad mood had disappeared completely. She and James dashed straight through to the residential unit at the back of the surgery. Simon, the practice nurse, was just settling a sleepy-looking rabbit into one of the empty cages.

Mandy proudly showed James the drake. 'Oh, he is lovely,' James said, admiring the bird as he looked out at them from the shelter of his cage. 'Wouldn't that make a fantastic photo? Look at the colour of his head!'

'He's looking a bit happier than he did this morning,' Mandy said. 'Did you manage to get all that fishing-line untangled, Simon?'

'Eventually,' he replied, running a hand through his spiky blond hair. 'It was quite a job, though – the line had been there for such a long time it had actually cut into his leg.' He shook his head. 'It's horrible stuff, nylon fishing-line. People ought to see the damage it causes.'

The drake gave a hoarse, low call and shifted uneasily. 'So what will happen to him now?' Mandy asked. 'Could he fend for himself if we put him back on a river or pond somewhere?' She knew that wild creatures should be kept in captivity for as short a time as possible.

'Your mother's got a plan,' Simon said, starting back towards the surgery. 'I haven't had a chance to ask her about it, but I know she's been fixing something up on the phone.'

'Simon! You're needed,' came a voice down the corridor, and then Emily Hope popped her head round the door. 'Hi, love,' she said, smiling at Mandy. 'And hello, James. What are you two up to?'

'Checking up on our duck,' Mandy answered. 'What's your plan for him, Mum?'

'Geraldine O'Meara,' her mother answered briefly, before she and Simon disappeared back to the surgery. 'I'll tell you all about it later,' she called over her shoulder as she went.

'So who's Geraldine O'Meara?' James asked, looking puzzled.

Mandy was smiling delightedly. 'Oh, come on, James! You remember,' she said. 'She's that journalist who writes for all the country magazines. You know, the one with the beagle and the tabby cat. I must have told you about the two of them!'

'Oh, yes, that does ring a bell,' James said, wandering off to inspect some of the other cages. 'They get on really well together, don't they?'

'They're devoted to each other,' Mandy said, taking one last look at the drake before following James. 'Robbie was the runt of the litter, and his mother abandoned him. Martha – she's the cat – had just had kittens, so she suckled Robbie too. He fed alongside the kittens, and Geraldine's convinced he still thinks Martha's his mother.'

'But why does your mother think Geraldine can help with the duck?' James said, watching a big lop-eared rabbit nibble on a piece of carrot.

'Geraldine has a pond on her smallholding,' Mandy answered. 'That must be what Mum has in mind – it would be the perfect spot for him.' She grabbed James's arm. 'Let's go through to the house. You can ring your mum and then, later on, we can persuade mine to take us with her when she goes to Geraldine's. You've got to come, James. Wood Vale is such an amazing place!'

'Now you're sure you can spare the time for this, Mandy?' Mrs Hope asked the next morning. She and Mandy were carefully loading the wire carrying-basket that held the drake into the back of the Land-rover. 'What about that project of yours?'

'Oh, Mum, I spent ages on it after breakfast,' Mandy said, slightly uneasily. She had spent ages *thinking* about the project, it was true, but her notebook was still only full of doodles. It was so difficult to choose the right topic – one that interested her but was scientific enough for Mr Marsh. *I'll have another go at it tomorrow*, she thought, putting biology firmly to the back of her mind.

'Bye, Dad!' she called from the passenger seat,

as Mr Hope's tall figure appeared in the cottage doorway to wave them off. 'See you later!'

They pulled out of the drive and into the lane. 'This is such a good idea of yours, Mum,' Mandy said, buckling up her safety belt. 'What made you think of Geraldine?'

'Well, I saw her with Martha in the surgery a couple of weeks ago,' Mrs Hope replied. 'She mentioned something then about the pond at Wood Vale. Then yesterday, it suddenly hit me that it would be the perfect place for Mr Duck. Luckily, when I phoned Geraldine she agreed at once. She's more than happy to keep an eye on him over the next few weeks.'

'Is Martha OK?' Mandy asked anxiously. 'Was it anything serious?'

'Just a case of conjunctivitis,' her mother said. 'Her eyes did look quite sore, but antibiotic drops should have cleared up the infection by now. She's getting quite an old lady,' she added in a gentler voice. 'Do you remember the very first time you saw her?'

'Only just,' Mandy replied, winding down the car window and taking in a deep breath of fresh air. It was a fine day in early summer, and all the village gardens were bright with sweet-smelling blossom. She screwed up her eyes and tried to focus on the memory. 'I think I remember Martha lying in her basket, with lots of furry little bodies next to her. It's all a bit hazy, though.'

'Well, you were only three,' said her mother, smoothing back a strand of curly auburn hair that the breeze had blown into her eyes. 'Just think – we've been looking after Geraldine's pets for over nine years now! I really don't know where the time goes.'

'Have you ever seen that happen before, Mum?' Mandy asked. 'A mother cat bringing up another baby animal, I mean.'

'Oh, yes, it's quite common,' Mrs Hope replied, braking as she steered round a sharp corner. 'Cats are such motherly creatures, they'll happily feed all sorts of orphans. I've even seen a newborn squirrel tucked in amongst a litter of kittens. But it *is* unusual that Robbie and Martha should still be so close now.'

Mandy smiled affectionately, thinking of all the times she'd seen the tabby patiently putting up with Robbie as he bounded around her. Once she'd caught Martha tapping him smartly on the nose when she was tired of the rough and tumble, but her claws were safely sheathed.

'Beagles are pack animals by nature,' her mother went on. 'But Robbie's quite different. Geraldine's often told me that he doesn't want to mix with other dogs – he'd much sooner be with Martha.' She grinned. 'They're like an old married couple.'

'Like you and Dad, you mean?' Mandy teased. 'I bet they don't argue all the time about who's going to do the washing-up!'

'Just as well it's your turn next, then,' said her mother promptly.

Mandy was about to protest when they turned into the Hunters' driveway, and James came out to meet them. His pet Labrador, Blackie, was rushing around his heels and Mr and Mrs Hunter had to stop him from jumping up into the Land-rover too.

The mallard gave a couple of quacks, as if asking whether they'd arrived. 'Not long now, Mr Duck,' Mandy said, turning round to check his cage was still wedged securely. 'Wait until you see your new home. You're going to love it!'

Twenty minutes later, they were driving along a winding lane that led steeply downhill. 'There it is!' Mandy cried, pointing back to a wooden sign nailed on to a huge yew tree at the side of the road. 'You've just gone past the gate, Mum.'

'Thanks, love,' her mother replied, reversing the Land-rover back a few metres. 'Why do I always manage to miss that turning? You'd think I'd know the way by now.'

Mandy jumped down to open the gate and her mother drove through. As the Land-rover crunched over the gravel drive, there was a volley of excited barking and a tan-and-white dog dashed out of the house to greet them. Mandy shut the gate behind her and hurried over to say hello, crouching down on her knees to give the beagle a big hug.

'This is Robbie,' she said, as James climbed out of the car to join them. 'He's gorgeous, isn't he?'

'Lovely,' James agreed, bending down and patting Robbie too. 'I think he can smell Blackie on me,' he added, as the beagle began sniffing his hand with great concentration and then licking it.

'You're always pleased to see visitors, aren't you, Robbie?' Mandy said, taking the dog's tawny head between her hands and gazing into his shining eyes while he wagged his tail furiously. He had a white muzzle, tapering up to a stripe between his eyes, and soft, toffee-coloured ears. His chest and legs were white, as was the tip of his jaunty tail, while the rest of his body was the same shade of caramel, splotched with darker patches of brown. Mandy particularly loved the way a furrow between Robbie's eyes sometimes made it look as though he was frowning, intent and busy, as he followed some enticing scent.

'I'd say you were quite a favourite, Mandy,' said a cheerful voice with a soft Irish lilt to it, and she looked up to see Geraldine O'Meara smiling down at her. 'But it must have been quite a while since you were last here,' she added, as Mandy jumped up to introduce James. 'I do believe you're taller than I am now!'

Geraldine might have been on the small side, but she was a bundle of energy. She reminded Mandy of a firework, fizzing with enthusiasm and never still for a minute. Her clear blue eyes always seemed to be sparkling with life. 'You only have to look at Geraldine to tell she's Irish,' Mandy's mum had said many times. 'Dark hair and pale skin, with those amazing blue eyes.' As usual, she was wearing a faded pair of jeans and a T-shirt. Today she'd topped them off with a pair of thigh-high waders, which were draped in pondweed.

'I hope we haven't caught you at a bad time,' Mrs Hope called, as she came over.

'Not at all,' Geraldine replied warmly, taking her hand and giving it a squeeze. 'It's always wonderful to see you! I was only checking over the pond to make sure it's all shipshape for our new guest. Let me just put Robbie inside while we take the mallard down there.'

'We'll see you in a minute, I promise!' Mandy

said, giving Robbie one last pat before he was taken away. Then she and James carefully slid the travelling cage out of the back of the Land-rover.

'Well, he doesn't look too much the worse for his journey,' Mrs Hope said, as the duck watched her steadily with his beady black eyes.

Geraldine closed the front door of the cottage safely behind her and came over to join them. She'd taken off her waders and replaced them with an old pair of trainers. 'Oh, that's a fine fellow,' she said, looking at the mallard. 'I think he'll do very well with us.'

'How many other ducks have you got at the moment?' Mandy asked, holding the cage securely, as she followed Geraldine through a side gate and into the back garden.

'There are five mallards, and their families,' Geraldine began, counting on her fingers as she led the way down a cobbled path between the trees. 'Two males and three females with six duck-lings. Plus a couple of tufted ducks I got in the spring.'

'What a fantastic place!' James exclaimed behind them. 'It looks like something out of a nature film.'

'See? I told you,' Mandy said, steadying the cage against her knee and turning back to grin at

James's wondering face as he gazed around.

The garden at Wood Vale looked like a clearing in some enchanted forest. Half of it was taken up by a large pond, fringed with reeds and bushes. A neatly-fenced vegetable patch lay opposite, and beyond that was a lawn the size of a small meadow, dotted with wild flowers among the grass. Some chickens wandered here and there, scratching at the ground, while others pecked busily in two large, wire-covered runs. The orchard stood on the other side of a bushy lavender hedge that ran along the far side of the garden.

'I'm glad you like it,' Geraldine said warmly. She stopped by a wooden bench close to a willow tree that looked out over the pond and added quietly, 'Most people thought I wouldn't be able to manage the place after my father died. I knew I could never sell it, though.'

Mandy settled the duck in his cage at her feet and followed Geraldine's gaze. A group of tall yellow irises were blooming among the rushes on the far side of the pond, and a rippling carpet of lilies opened their creamy white flowers on the quiet water. She could understand just how Geraldine felt. If Wood Vale belonged to her family, she wouldn't want to leave either.

Noticing James's puzzled expression, Geraldine

explained, 'I grew up at Wood Vale, but my mother died when I was quite young. Ten years ago my father became ill, so I moved back home to look after him. And here I am still!'

'Making a wonderful job of it, too,' Mrs Hope put in, sitting down on the bench. 'Oh, look, Mandy! James! Over there!' She pointed to a couple of mallards who had just emerged from a clump of rushes, followed by a bobbing line of fluffy ducklings.

'Come on, everyone!' Mandy said, suddenly reminded of why they were there. 'Let's set this poor old duck free. I bet he can't wait to get his feet wet again.'

'Of course! Whatever am I thinking of, rambling on like this!' Geraldine exclaimed, tearing her eyes away from the pond and looking down at the drake. 'And why did I take my waders off? I'll just nip back to the house and get them. Then I can take his cage down to the water and let him come out in his own time.'

'Don't worry!' Mandy said, kicking off her canvas shoes. 'I'll do it.' She rolled up the legs of her jeans and scrambled down to the edge of the pond with the cage in her arms. Soft, silky mud oozed between her toes. 'Here you are, Mr Duck,' she said, setting the cage down and opening the front flap. 'Welcome to paradise!'

The mallard gave another of his low, husky calls. For a while he stayed still, staring out as though he couldn't believe his eyes. After a moment, he moved forward slowly, one step at a time, his bad leg dragging behind. Mandy held her breath. The drake paused for a second at the mouth of the cage. Then, with a stream of hoarse quacks, he sailed out on to the water, looking all around with what she thought was a very satisfied expression.

'Success!' she called to the others, swinging the empty cage and making her way back up the bank to join them. She wiped her feet on the springy grass and jammed her shoes back on. They all watched as their duck stretched his wings with a whir and a flap, then started busily searching for food.

'He can swim just fine,' James observed. 'His leg doesn't seem to bother him at all in the water.'

'Will the other ducks accept him?' Mandy asked Geraldine.

'I think they should,' she replied. 'Now if it was swans we were dealing with, that would be a very different matter. They're much more territorial – won't accept a stranger on their patch.'

A few minutes later, their mallard had joined the

other ducks on the pond, and Mandy had to look carefully to tell him apart.

'Of course, he'll be losing that glossy green head very soon,' Geraldine said, shading her eyes with one hand as she stared into the sun.

'What do you mean?' Mandy asked in alarm. 'Will the others pick on him? I thought you said they'd be OK?'

'It's nothing like that, to be sure,' Geraldine said, laughing as she put her arm round Mandy's waist. 'No, he's going to be losing his feathers – moulting! He'll look much more like the females in a month or so, and he won't be able to fly. The experts call it "being in eclipse".'

'I'm sure he'll have settled in by then,' Mandy said, watching as the ducks set off in stately procession towards a clump of bright green weed. 'He won't want to go anywhere else.'

'Well now, everything looks fine on the duck front,' Geraldine said briskly, turning away from the water. 'So you can all come along to the orchard with me.' She stretched out a hand to pull Emily Hope up from the bench and declared, 'There's something I want to show you – and I promise it's worth seeing!'

Mandy took one last look at the pond and then followed the others over the long grass with a spring in her step. The drake seemed happily settled, and she couldn't wait to discover what Geraldine had in store. She usually had some new scheme on the go, which she would write about for the country magazines she worked on. Added to that, Robbie and Martha were waiting for them up at the house. In fact, the day seemed pretty much perfect, so far!

Three

'Here we are!' Geraldine said, throwing out one arm with a flourish. 'My newest exciting enterprise!'

Mandy and James looked towards the patch of rough ground at the edge of the orchard, and then back at each other. 'What exactly are those?' Mandy said uncertainly. She didn't want to disappoint Geraldine, but she didn't have a clue what the two small wooden houses were for.

And then James let out a cry. 'Beehives!' he said. 'That's what they are, aren't they? Look, you can see a couple of bees flying around the roof.'

'They are indeed,' Geraldine said proudly. 'By next year, Wood Vale Organic Honey should be up and running. Isn't that wonderful?'

'Fantastic,' Mandy agreed politely, but without much enthusiasm. She was rather wary of bees, and she'd been expecting something quite different – a couple of goats in the orchard perhaps, or even a pony, or a nice fat pig who could rootle about under the trees. You couldn't exactly bond with a bee, could you?

'Oh, get away with you!' Geraldine said, taking Mandy's arm and gently pushing her forward. 'You can do better than that, Mandy Hope! Come and have a look. When I've told you what amazing creatures bees are, you'll understand why I'm so excited. Don't worry – we won't get too close.'

'OK,' Mandy said, prepared to give Geraldine the benefit of the doubt. 'And you come too, Mum,' she added, pulling Emily Hope along with them. It wasn't that she was frightened exactly, but she did feel a bit nervous.

James was already standing at a safe distance opposite one of the hives. 'So what's going on in there?' he asked Geraldine. 'I can see the bees going in by that little entrance. . .' and he pointed to a tiny hole above a wooden shelf at the base of the hive, '. . .but I don't know what they're up to inside.'

'Those are some worker bees,' Geraldine told

them. 'They've been off looking for flower nectar to bring back to the hive. Now, inside, there are other worker bees making honeycomb out of wax. The queen bee will laying an egg in each of the cells of the honeycomb. And can you guess how many eggs she can lay in a day? Go on, have a go.'

'Twenty?' Mandy tried, interested almost in spite of herself. Geraldine shook her head. 'All right then, fifty,' Mandy guessed again. 'No, make that a hundred.'

'*Two thousand!*' Geraldine told them, her eyes shining. 'Isn't that amazing?'

'Wow!' James breathed, pushing his glasses back up his nose as he peered forward. 'She must be worn out.'

'She has attendants to look after her,' Geraldine said, putting her hands in her pockets and leaning back as she watched the bees coming and going. 'They feed her and groom her, while other bees look after the grubs as they hatch. Oh, I can't tell you how fascinating it is, once you start learning how the hive works.'

'So what about the honey?' Mandy asked, coming nearer to the hives and standing next to James. 'How's that made? And where is it, exactly?'

'Well, the worker bees come back to the hive with pollen and nectar, and water too,' Geraldine said. 'It all gets mixed up in their honey stomachs, and then they seal it in other cells in the honeycomb and leave it to ripen.'

'Do you talk to your bees, Geraldine?' asked Emily Hope with a smile. 'Don't the old country folk say you should talk to them and tell them all your news?'

'Would you believe, I do talk to them,' she confessed, looking slightly embarrassed. 'I know it's crazy, though. Bees can't hear,' she explained to Mandy and James. 'They communicate through smell and vibration.'

'How, exactly?' James asked. He was always keen to find out the precise facts behind any statement.

'Just listen to this,' Geraldine began, her face alight with interest. 'When a worker bee finds a new source of nectar – say my lavender bushes have started to bloom – she comes back to the hive and does a special dance on the side of the honeycomb. It tells the others precisely where the nectar is – how far away *and* in what direction. And of course they can smell the pollen on her too, so that helps them find it.'

'That's incredible!' Mandy said. 'Hey!' She took a couple of quick steps backwards, as a bee buzzed a little too close to her face for comfort.

'Maybe it's time for a cup of tea,' Geraldine said,

laughing and putting an arm round her shoulder. 'I could talk about bees for hours, but I'm sure Robbie's wondering what we're up to. Still, I hope I've whetted your appetite.'

James nodded enthusiastically, and Mandy had to agree. There *was* something fascinating about bees, even if they weren't particularly cuddly.

'And how's Martha doing?' Mandy asked Geraldine, as they walked up the path towards the house. 'Has her conjunctivitis cleared up?'

Geraldine frowned slightly and jammed her hands in the pockets of her jeans. 'It's better than it was,' she said. 'She's not quite herself, though – she doesn't seem to want to do anything much. Still, I suppose that's normal for an old cat like her.' She looked at Mandy and summoned up a smile. 'Why don't you give her a look over, and tell me what you think.'

'Of course I will,' Mandy replied, worried by the sad look in Geraldine's eyes. 'And even better, so will Mum. Her bag's in the Land-rover.'

Geraldine was about to say something else, when a volley of loud barks sounded from inside the house. 'Would you listen to that!' she said. 'Somebody's feeling left out.'

She opened the back door and immediately Robbie bounded towards them, only pausing for a second to pick up a rubber ball that was lying in the flower-bed. He dropped it at Mandy's feet, looking up at her appealingly and wagging his tail.

'All right,' Mandy said, smiling. 'Just one quick throw, OK?' She had such a soft spot for Robbie, and it was impossible to resist his dark, shining eyes. He was a beautiful-looking dog but, on top of that, there was a sweetness in his nature that made him extra special. Although she'd often seen him teasing Martha, frisking around her and nuzzling her with his nose, he was always careful not to hurt her. And he was so affectionate! Mandy knew that as soon as she sat down, Robbie would be next to her, trying to snuggle up as close as possible and laying his head on her lap.

'You'll be here all day now,' Geraldine laughed from the doorstep, as Mandy threw the ball in a wide arc over the vegetable patch and on to the grass beyond. Robbie tore off down the path in hot pursuit.

'Can you take over now, James?' Mandy asked. She was anxious to have a look at Martha as soon as possible.

'Sure,' he replied, before whistling Robbie back, so that Mandy could follow her mother and Geraldine through the back door.

It was easy to tell from the state of the kitchen

that Geraldine was more interested in the garden at Wood Vale than she was in the house. Mandy liked the shabby, comfortable feel of the room, though. Everything looked old and well used. Pots and pans were hooked on to a circular rack that hung down from the ceiling, and a huge wooden dresser held Geraldine's collection of china, in every colour under the rainbow. The walls were covered in framed black-and-white photographs of the O'Meara family, while more recent colour snaps took up every centimetre of space between.

Mandy usually enjoyed looking at the photos, but today she went straight over to a large wicker basket in one corner of the kitchen. 'Hello there, Martha,' she said softly, crouching down to stroke the grey tabby cat who was lying there asleep. Immediately, she could tell that Martha had lost weight. The cat's ribs and knobbly spine stuck out prominently.

Martha opened her eyes, and Mandy could see that her eyelids were red and inflamed. 'You don't look very happy, poor old girl,' she murmured to Martha, scratching her behind the ears. The tabby pushed her head against Mandy's fingers, and then closed her eyes again.

Mandy looked over to where her mother was standing, leaning against the dresser and watching her, while Geraldine filled the kettle and put it on

her ancient stove. Something in Mandy's expression must have showed her alarm, because Mrs Hope came over to the basket straight away. She took one look at Martha and then gently lifted her out. 'Do you mind if I give Martha a quick examination, Geraldine?' she asked, setting the cat down on a newspaper that was lying on the kitchen table. 'Perhaps you could hold her for a minute while I wash my hands?'

'Of course,' Geraldine replied, going over to the table. 'Soap's in the dish and there's a towel hanging up by the door.' When she saw Martha, she added worriedly, 'Oh dear, oh dear. She looks much worse all of a sudden. Why didn't I check up on her more often? I just got so carried away with the pond, and then the bees and everything. . .'

'I'll get your bag from the Land-rover, Mum,' Mandy offered. She felt a cold hand clutch at her stomach as she hurried through the house and out of the front door to the car. They'd been so carefree before – now all she could think about was what might be wrong with Martha.

By the time she returned to the kitchen, James was standing by the table too, with Robbie next to him. He shot her an anxious look, while the beagle sniffed at Martha's feet and whined quietly.

'Here you are, Mum,' Mandy said, putting the bag down on the table and then going to wash her hands in the sink too, in case she was needed to help.

'Thanks, love,' Mrs Hope murmured, probing Martha's stomach gently with her fingers. 'She's certainly very thin,' she went on, turning to Geraldine. 'How's her appetite?'

Geraldine shook her head. 'She hasn't been eating much for the last couple of days,' she said, running one hand through her mop of dark curls and frowning again.

Martha stood on the kitchen table with her legs bent and her tail lowered. Mrs Hope carefully opened the cat's mouth, looked at her teeth and gums, and took her temperature. Robbie barked a couple of times and looked inquiringly up at Mandy, as though asking what was going on.

'Don't worry,' she told him. 'We're just trying to find out what's the matter with Martha, that's all.'

'We won't hurt her,' James added, patting Robbie reassuringly.

'Could you pass me a syringe, please, Mandy?' her mother said, while she waited for Martha's temperature to register. 'I'd like to take a blood sample,' she explained to Geraldine. 'That'll be the most accurate way of finding out exactly what's the matter with Martha. I'd sooner not make a diagnosis until I'm absolutely sure, and it won't take long. I can run the test myself back at Animal Ark and have the results the next day.'

'Of course,' Geraldine replied distractedly. 'Whatever needs to be done. I'm so sorry – I should have brought her in to see you before now, obviously. I just thought she might have had a touch of cat flu. She does get it now and then, but she usually manages to shake it off after a day or so.'

Mandy located a syringe in the bag and removed the sterile cover, before passing it to her mother.

Mrs Hope was looking at Martha's temperature

on the thermometer, but her face gave nothing away. 'Don't be too hard on yourself,' she said to Geraldine while she took the blood sample. 'Martha could have taken a turn for the worse with very little warning.'

'I'm sure Mum will be able to sort everything out,' Mandy added sympathetically. She knew how much Geraldine loved Martha, and she could imagine just how awful she was feeling.

'Right! All done,' said Mrs Hope, after she'd finished by giving Martha an antibiotic injection. 'I'll leave you some antibiotics and eye drops, and here's a sample pack of some liquid food that you might like to try her with. Perhaps you could pop her back in the basket now, Mandy?'

'Sure,' Mandy said, picking Martha up as carefully as she could. Immediately Robbie whirled around and dashed over to the basket, settling himself in it and looking up at her. 'Hey, Robbie!' Mandy exclaimed. 'Don't you think you should let Martha have the best place?'

'That's exactly what he's doing,' Geraldine said. She came over to stand beside them, and Mandy saw that there was a tear on her cheek. 'Martha likes to sleep next to him,' she explained, dashing one hand quickly over her eyes and then giving a wan smile. 'Robbie takes his duties very seriously, you know. He's just getting into the right position.'

'Well. . .' Mandy began doubtfully. Surely if Martha were ill, it would be better for her not to be with Robbie in the basket? She looked over to the sink, where her mother was washing her hands. But Mrs Hope quickly nodded her head.

'OK, you're the boss,' Mandy said. She lowered Martha's thin little body carefully into the basket. Immediately, the cat curled herself into a neat ball against Robbie's clean white stomach and closed her eyes. Gently, he licked her ear a couple of times and then laid his own head next to hers, forming a protective curve round her body.

Geraldine looked tenderly at them both, and then tucked a faded soft toy between Robbie's paws. 'Mouse has to go in the basket too,' she confessed, with an embarrassed smile.

'Just like an old married couple,' Emily Hope repeated, walking over and putting a comforting arm round Mandy's shoulder.

Mandy tried to reply, but the lump in her throat made it difficult to speak. *Oh, please, let Martha get better!* she said silently to herself.

Four

'Have you got any idea what *might* be the matter with Martha?' Mandy asked her mother worriedly, after they'd waved goodbye to Geraldine and pulled out of the drive at Wood Vale.

'Well, I didn't want to say anything to Geraldine until we know for sure,' Mrs Hope said slowly, 'but I've got a strong suspicion that Martha might have FIV – Feline Immunodeficiency Virus, to give the condition its full name. Quite a mouthful, isn't it?'

'What's that, exactly?' Mandy asked. 'Is it serious?' The nagging sense of worry in the pit of her stomach was growing stronger by the second.

'Yes, it is, I'm afraid,' Mrs Hope admitted, as she drove the Land-rover slowly up the steep hill. 'FIV affects the immune system, you see. It makes cats more prone to other infections that they haven't the strength to shake off – like Martha's conjunctivitis.'

'Poor Martha,' James said, sitting back. 'But how would she catch FIV in the first place?'

'Well, it's spread through body fluids – so probably from saliva,' Mrs Hope explained. 'Martha might have been bitten by an infected cat at some time or other. The virus could have been in her system for a while before she developed any symptoms. Unfortunately, there's no vaccination against it.'

'So what happens now?' Mandy asked her mother. 'How do we treat her?'

By now, they had reached the top of the lane and were waiting to join the main road. Emily Hope put on the handbrake for a moment and laid a hand over Mandy's. 'There isn't a cure for FIV,' she said gently, a sympathetic look in her green eyes. 'We can treat the secondary infections Martha's developed with antibiotics, but there's no getting rid of the virus itself. If she *does* have FIV, that is. We can't be certain until her blood's been tested.'

'But you're pretty sure she has,' Mandy said miserably. 'You wouldn't have mentioned it to us otherwise.' She felt tears beginning to prickle at the back of her eyes. She'd known Martha for most of her life. It was awful to think of the motherly tabby cat being so ill – and beyond their help, too. 'Surely there must be something we can do for her?' she added fiercely, quickly brushing her eyes with the back of her hand.

'We can make sure she doesn't suffer too much pain,' her mother said, looking to her left and right before edging the Land-rover out into the road. 'Martha's had a long and happy life, after all. Between us, we'll be able to give her a peaceful and dignified end.'

Mandy stared out of the window without taking in what she was seeing. It was almost unbearable to imagine Robbie lying all alone in the basket, with no Martha to cuddle up against him.

Nobody said very much for the rest of the journey back to Welford.

'Come on now, love,' Mrs Hope said, breaking the silence as they approached the village. 'Try not to get too sad and mopey. That won't do any good, will it?' And she patted Mandy's knee.

'I suppose not,' Mandy said, giving herself a little shake and doing her best to cheer up. She tried to think of something that might stop her brooding. 'Could James stay for supper tonight?' she asked her mother. 'Perhaps we could go out for a pizza or something.'

'Good idea!' Mrs Hope replied. 'What do you say, James?'

'That would be great,' James said enthusiastically. 'I don't think I can stay very late, though. We're visiting my gran tomorrow, and we have to get up early.'

'I'll give your parents a ring as soon as we get in and tell them we'll be sure to drop you back in good time,' Mandy's mother promised as they walked up the path to the cottage. Then she stopped and sniffed the air. 'Hang on, we may have to hold that pizza,' she added. 'I think Dad's started cooking already.' A savoury smell had come wafting out to greet them.

'Just so long as it's not cabbage soup,' Mandy groaned. Her father was always trying to lose weight and keep fit. He'd made so much cabbage soup for his latest diet that Mandy and her mum had eventually protested. 'If I eat another bowl of cabbage soup, I'm going to start turning green!' Emily Hope had said.

'You haven't gone back on your word, have you, Dad?' Mandy asked, once they were all in the cosy, oak-beamed kitchen. 'You're not by any chance making something that begins with C and S?' She looked at him sternly and folded her arms.

'Now what could that possibly be?' Mr Hope replied, his eyes twinkling as he scratched his dark beard and tried not to smile. He was wearing an apron and his face was flushed with heat from the stove. 'Cheese soufflé, perhaps? Or chop suey? Chicken stew, maybe? No, it's none of those.' Then he stopped frowning and put on a pained expression. 'Surely you can't mean my tasty cabbage soup? But I bet James would just love to try some!'

'Dad!' Mandy warned, poking him with a wooden spoon. 'You promised. . .'

'Don't worry! I've decided cabbage soup's too good for you lot.' Her father grinned, turning back to the hob and stirring a bubbling saucepan. 'You'll have to make do with vegetable lasagne instead. I'll just have to go for a jog tomorrow and work it all off.'

'Sounds perfect!' Mrs Hope said, giving her husband a quick hug. 'I'll go and ring the Hunters quickly to see whether James can stay. Mandy, you need to clear all those books off the kitchen table, please, so we can start laying it.'

'You know, I've had an idea,' James confided, as he helped Mandy tidy the books back into her schoolbag. 'I was thinking about Geraldine in the

Land-rover just now, and I wondered whether you might want to write about bees for your project. I thought they were fascinating, didn't you?'

Mandy stood still for a moment with a file clutched against her chest as she considered his suggestion. 'You're brilliant!' she exclaimed after a few seconds' thought, her eyes shining with enthu-siasm. 'Geraldine can tell me all about them, and I can make it really scientific. We've done pollination in class already. Thanks, James! You're a superstar!'

'That's all right,' James said, blushing to the roots of his hair as he stuffed a couple of textbooks into the bag. 'I'm glad you think it could work.'

'Mum's visiting Geraldine tomorrow to see how Martha is,' Mandy went on. 'I wanted to go with her anyway. Perhaps I could talk to Geraldine about it then. I bet she's got some books I could borrow.'

But Mrs Hope looked doubtful when Mandy explained the plan to her over supper. 'I don't know, love,' she said. 'We should have the results of Martha's blood test by tomorrow. If it's bad news, I'll need to break it to Geraldine and discuss Martha's treatment with her. I think she might have other things on her mind apart from bees, don't you?'

'Maybe,' Mandy admitted, chasing a slice of

carrot round her plate. Perhaps it would be insensitive to expect Geraldine to help with her project at such a difficult time. It was a pity, though. James had suggested the ideal subject and she couldn't wait to get started. Mr Marsh would be furious if she hadn't done any research, and although she and James had searched through all the books in the study, they'd only found one short paragraph about bees.

She tried to think back to what Geraldine had told them that afternoon, but it wasn't enough to build up a whole picture. And then she remembered Geraldine's look of pride and enthusiasm as she'd shown them the hives. What had she said? 'I could talk about bees for hours.' That was it. And she'd seemed so forlorn as they left, turning to go back into the house.

'I don't know,' she began slowly. 'I got the feeling this afternoon that Geraldine was rather lonely. She was so pleased to see us, and do you remember how keen she was that we stayed for tea? She might be glad of some company tomorrow – especially if there *is* bad news about Martha.'

'You may have a point there,' Mr Hope said, waving his fork at her and sending a piece of lettuce flying across the table. 'I've often thought how isolated Wood Vale must be for someone as lively as

Geraldine. I know she's got lots of friends, but there's no one close by for her to call on.'

'Besides,' James put in, 'she knows so much about bees. Helping Mandy with her project might be just what she needs to take her mind off things.'

'Well, you could be right,' Mrs Hope said, putting her knife and fork together and sitting back. 'Geraldine's certainly the kind of person who likes to be busy doing something, rather than sitting around brooding. Why don't you come along with me tomorrow then, Mandy, and we'll see what she says about it.'

Mandy began to collect up the empty plates, thinking about what the next day might hold. Tomorrow they would find out for certain whether her mother's diagnosis was right. If it was, they would have sad news to bring to Wood Vale.

It took Mandy a long time to get to sleep that night, and she didn't wake up until much later than usual on Sunday morning. By the time she'd got dressed and gone downstairs for breakfast, her mother was already coming out of the surgery. Mandy took one look at her face and realised the news wasn't good.

'It's just as I thought, I'm afraid,' her mother said sadly, shaking her head. 'Martha's blood shows she does have FIV, and she's extremely anaemic too. No wonder she's very thin and weak.'

Mandy put down the cereal packet, her appetite suddenly gone. She felt so sorry for Martha – and for Geraldine and Robbie, too. 'We'd better go over there right away,' she said to her mother, getting up from the table.

'When you've had something to eat,' Mrs Hope replied firmly, putting a hand on Mandy's shoulder and pushing her gently back down in the chair. 'You can't do anything useful on an empty stomach. Besides,' she added, looking at her watch, 'Geraldine's not expecting us for another hour or so yet.'

When they arrived at Wood Vale a little while later, it took Geraldine a few minutes to answer their knock at the door. She was looking pale and anxious, quite different from her usual cheerful self. Robbie was overjoyed to see them, though. He bounded around their heels, barking excitedly and wagging his tail.

'How's our patient?' Mrs Hope asked, as Geraldine took them through to the kitchen.

'Not good,' she replied. 'I've given her some of that liquid food you left yesterday, and the antibiotics, of course, but she doesn't want to get up. I took her basket down to the pond this morning so she could lie in the sun for a while, and she seemed to like that.' She smiled, looking down at Martha, who was still curled up in the basket, and added, 'It's her favourite spot, you know, sitting with Robbie at the foot of the willow tree and looking out over the water.'

'Well, at least her eyes are looking better,' Mrs Hope said. She rose to her feet and put an arm round Geraldine's shoulder. 'Come and sit down,' she went on. 'I've got the results of Martha's blood test. We need to talk about her illness, and how to treat it.'

Mandy stayed where she was, crouching down by the basket and scratching Martha comfortingly behind the ears. She knew what her mother was going to say, and she didn't feel like hearing it all over again. Robbie sat next to her, resting his head against her side.

From time to time, phrases floated over from the kitchen table. She heard her mother say '. . . no resistance to infection. . . can only treat the symptoms. . . make her as comfortable as possible. . .' and Geraldine's soft Irish voice murmuring something she couldn't quite catch. Eventually she couldn't bear only hearing snippets of the conversation and got up to join them. Robbie followed close behind.

Geraldine's eyes were red and she was blowing her nose on a tissue. 'Would you look at me being so foolish!' she told Mandy with a watery smile. 'Anyone would think I'd expected Martha to live for ever. It's just that we'll miss her so much. Won't we, Robbie?' And she buried her face in the beagle's silky coat.

'Of course you will!' Mandy exclaimed, biting her lip as she tried hard not to cry too. If *she* was feeling miserable, it must be a hundred times worse for Geraldine – and for poor Robbie, who had no idea what was happening to Martha. 'I just wish there was something we could do,' she added unhappily.

'Oh, but you've done so much already,' Geraldine replied, straightening up and blowing her nose again. Then she looked almost fearfully at Mandy's mother. 'Unless you think the time's come. . .?'

'No, I don't think Martha's in so much pain we should put her to sleep,' Mrs Hope replied. 'We'll carry on with the antibiotics for the moment and see how things go. I'll come and see her as often as you want me to.' She gave Mandy a quick glance and added, 'And now perhaps we should leave you in peace, Geraldine.'

'Oh no, don't go yet!' Geraldine said at once,

jumping to her feet. 'You must stay for a cup of tea, at least! Or why don't we all have an early lunch? Please, I'd like that. And besides, I haven't even taken you down to the pond to show you how that fine drake's getting on.'

She genuinely seemed to want them to stay, and Mandy was certain her gut feeling had been right. Geraldine would much sooner have their company than be left on her own.

Her mother seemed to be thinking on the same lines. 'The trouble is, I've got a pile of paperwork at home I need to catch up on,' she said. 'But I know Mandy's been wondering if she could talk to you about something.'

'Of course,' Geraldine said, tucking the tissue away in her sleeve. 'Fire away, Mandy. Ask me anything you like.'

'Well, we have to do a project at school, for biology,' Mandy began, not quite sure if Geraldine was really ready for such a quick change of subject. She was looking at Mandy expectantly, though, so she decided to press on. 'We thought it was so interesting yesterday – everything you were telling us about your bees, that is. James suggested I should write about them, and I wondered if you—'

'Oh, Mandy, I'd love to help!' Geraldine beamed. 'There's so much I can tell you – all about how the hive is organised, and the different jobs the bees have, and how they make honey. And I've got a couple of excellent books you can borrow. We could get started right away!'

'That's settled, then,' Mrs Hope smiled, as she kneeled by the basket to say goodbye to Martha. 'If you're sure it's OK with you, Geraldine, I could leave Mandy here and pick her up in a couple of hours.'

After Mrs Hope had gone and Geraldine had given Martha a quick cuddle, she took Mandy through to her study. 'Right,' she said briskly. 'Before you start writing anything down, why don't I explain how the hive works and show you those books I mentioned? If there's anything you don't understand, just ask me.'

Mandy was delighted. It was lovely to sit in the quiet, sunny room, with Robbie asleep at her feet, and listen to Geraldine talk. She had the knack of explaining things so clearly that Mandy hardly ever had to interrupt. Geraldine had given her a pad of paper to take notes if she wanted, but Mandy was so absorbed in what she was saying that she forgot to write anything down.

After what seemed hardly any time at all, Geraldine looked at her watch and exclaimed, 'Oh, you poor thing! I've been talking at you for

nearly an hour. Why don't we have a break now?'
She reached up and took a couple of books down
from the shelf. 'Here,' she added, handing them to
Mandy, 'have a look at these while I go and make
us a sandwich. You must be starving.' And she hurried off to the kitchen, Robbie trotting hopefully
along with her.

Mandy was browsing through the books when, a few minutes later, Geraldine came bursting back into the study. Her face was chalky white. 'Oh, Mandy, I think we'd better ring your mother right away,' she gasped in a panicky voice. 'Martha's in a bad way. Please, come and see!'

Five

Mandy looked anxiously into the basket. Martha was still lying curled on her side, but her breathing had become very uneven. She seemed to be taking much longer inward breaths than normal and struggling to breathe out again. She looked very ill indeed.

'You're right, I think we should phone Mum immediately,' Mandy said to Geraldine, who was kneeling beside her.

'I'll go and ring right now,' Geraldine said, jumping to her feet. 'Can you stay with Martha? I don't want her to be on her own.'

'Of course,' Mandy replied. She tried to think what she could do to help in the meantime. Perhaps

She should check Martha's heart rate – that might be useful for her mother to know. She'd done this before. It was just a question of finding the right spot to feel the heartbeat. At last she located a rapid, faint fluttering on the left-hand side of Martha's chest, behind her elbow. She looked at her watch and tried to count the beats for fifteen seconds. The pulse rate was dangerously fast.

'Your mum's on her way,' Geraldine said, coming back into the kitchen and crouching down again by the basket. She stroked Martha gently and murmured, 'Hold on, old girl.'

Robbie had pushed his way in between Mandy and Geraldine. He nudged the basket with his nose and whined, as though wondering what was the matter with Martha.

'You must be very gentle now,' Mandy told him. 'Martha's not feeling so good.'

Robbie gazed up at her with his deep brown eyes. He gave a short bark and then turned round, padding purposefully across the kitchen. Pausing by the back door, he gave another urgent bark and looked at Mandy again. 'Do you want to go out?' she asked him, tearing her eyes away from Martha. 'OK, I'm just coming.' Geraldine was there to keep the tabby company, so she might as well make herself useful.

She opened the door for Robbie and he bounded off down the garden path, making straight for the pond. Mandy watched curiously as he sniffed around by the willow tree. It looked as though he were searching for something. Then suddenly his body stiffened and his tail wagged excitedly. He barked again and pushed his muzzle into the long grass, then turned around with something in his mouth and trotted back up the path.

'What have you got there?' Mandy said curiously, as she let him into the kitchen again. She couldn't quite see what he was holding so carefully. 'Hey, come back!' she called anxiously as he pushed past her.

'It's all right,' Geraldine said, as Robbie dropped his offering into the basket. 'Look! He's found Mouse.' And she held up the shabby soft toy Martha loved.

'Mouse must have fallen out of the basket this morning,' Geraldine said, a catch in her voice, 'I hadn't even realised she was missing. But you knew, didn't you, Robbie?' She stroked the beagle's ear.

'There's a clever boy,' Mandy exclaimed, hurrying over and crouching down to give Robbie a hug. The beagle looked at her with such a hopeful expression, she could hardly bear it. *I've done what*

I can, he seemed to be saying. *Now it's up to you two to make Martha better.*

Geraldine put the faded stuffed mouse between Martha's paws. The old cat opened her eyes for a second and focused on the worn, grey material, before closing them wearily again. And then Robbie put his head into the basket they shared and gently began to lick her thin body.

Mandy looked at Geraldine, uncertain whether they should allow him to carry on. Geraldine shrugged and raised her eyebrows. 'He seems to be helping her relax,' she murmured.

It was true. Martha was taking in air much more naturally now and she wasn't fighting to breathe out again, either. Then gradually, Mandy became aware of a faint rumbling sound coming from Martha's chest as Robbie carefully massaged it with his clean pink tongue.

'Geraldine!' she said softly, nudging her side. 'Martha can't be purring, can she?'

'She is, bless her!' Geraldine whispered, her blue eyes brighter than ever with tears. 'Who'd have believed it?'

A weak, rusty purr hung on the air for a few seconds longer. Then slowly the sound slowly faded away until Mandy could no longer hear a trace of it, no matter how hard she strained to listen.

Robbie stopped licking and sank down beside the basket, his head between his paws.

'She's gone, hasn't she?' Geraldine whispered, the tears spilling down on to her cheeks.

Mandy nodded wordlessly. She felt for Martha's heartbeat again, just in case there was a chance she was still alive. In her heart, though, she knew it was hopeless.

'I'll go and wait for Mum outside,' she said, getting heavily to her feet. Geraldine and Robbie would want to say a last goodbye to their old friend.

Mandy slept badly again that night. She'd begun to write a plan for her project when they came back from Geraldine's, even though it really wasn't what she felt like doing, and her mind wouldn't stop racing when it was time for bed. Besides the bees, she couldn't help thinking about everything that had happened that day, and worrying about Geraldine and Robbie. She'd rung James that evening and broken the sad news about Martha. His class – which was the year below Mandy's – was going on a geography trip on Monday, and she wanted to tell him what had happened as soon as she could.

Luckily, Mr Hope was going through Walton the next morning. After taking one look at the dark shadows under Mandy's eyes, he offered to give her a lift to school. Mandy yawned as she unpacked her schoolbag in the classroom. They had double English first – that wasn't so bad – and biology after break. Then her hand flew up to her face and she groaned. The outline plan for her biology project was still lying on the kitchen table at home. Mr Marsh would kill her!

When she made her confession to him at the start of the lesson, Mr Marsh looked as though that was exactly what he felt like doing. 'I can't believe you haven't brought in your outline!' he exploded. 'Have you forgotten everything we talked about last week already? You probably haven't even begun your project.'

'Oh, but I have!' Mandy exclaimed, feeling outraged. After all the work she'd done yesterday! 'I
decided to write about bees,' she went on, feeling
the colour rise in her cheeks, 'and I've drawn up a
really detailed plan of the whole thing. Honestly!'

She had to stop talking at that point, because
she could feel a big lump forming in her throat.
There was no way she was going to cry in front of
Mr Marsh – she'd sooner die!

He looked at her for a few seconds without
speaking. Then he said, a little more calmly,
'That's not a bad choice. Well, I'll look forward to
seeing your outline tomorrow. I'll check it over as
soon as I can and you'll just have to get on with
your project in the meantime. But I'm going to
have to give you a detention for Friday, Amanda.
You've left me with no alternative!'

'Yes, Mr Marsh. Sorry, sir,' Mandy muttered, too
tired to argue. As she turned to go back to her
desk, she felt as though things couldn't get any
worse.

The day seemed to drag on for ever, and even
when her dad appeared at the end of it to give
Mandy a lift home, it didn't lift her spirits. They
drove along in silence for a while, until Mr Hope
suddenly smiled.

'I know what might cheer you up,' he said.

'We've got a new arrival in the residential unit. Or should I say, arrivals?'

'Oh? Who?' Mandy asked, making an effort to shake herself out of this dark mood.

'Wait and see,' her father replied. 'It'll be worth it!' He wouldn't say any more, no matter how much Mandy nagged. As soon as the Land-rover arrived at Animal Ark, she hurried through the surgery to the residential unit.

'Oh, isn't that wonderful?' she breathed, looking into one of the cages.

A beautiful chocolate-brown Burmese cat was lying in a blanket-lined box, fast asleep. Four tiny kittens lay sprawled against her stomach in a tangled heap. Their eyes were shut tight, and they looked only a few hours old.

Mandy gazed at the little family in delight. She always found newborn animals particularly special. 'They're absolutely gorgeous,' she said, taking in every detail of the kittens' damp, tousled bodies. Their thin, fragile legs were like twigs, and the fur was still sparse over their pink skin. As she watched, one of the kittens gave a reedy mew and began to struggle blindly towards its mother's teat. She opened one golden eye and helped nudge it into place with her nose.

'I thought you'd like to see them,' said Mr

Hope. He put an arm round Mandy's shoulder and added quietly, 'The miracle of new life. It helps make up for the sad times, doesn't it?'

'Yes, it does,' said Mandy, resting her hand on his. This time the tears in her eyes were happy ones. 'Is anything wrong with them, Dad?' she added, turning to her father with a suddenly anxious look. 'Why are they here?'

'Don't worry, they're fine,' he replied. 'We had to perform a Caesarean on their mother this morning, that's all. She's not a big cat, and we thought she wouldn't be able to deliver the kittens alone. Those three males might look small, but they're actually quite hefty for newborns.'

'Will they turn darker brown, like their mother?' Mandy asked. Two of the kittens were a soft fawn colour, one was a darker grey, and the smallest of the litter had a pale, creamy coat.

'Well, their father was a blue Burmese,' Mr Hope said. 'I think those two males will be chocolate and that one blue, like his dad. The little female looks as though she'll be lilac, though. That's a sort of silvery, pinky grey – quite beautiful.' He watched the litter for a moment and then added, 'We're going to have to keep an eye on her, I think.'

'Oh, why?' Mandy asked, looking at the tiny

kitten at the end of the row.

'Her brothers seem intent on pushing her out,' Mr Hope replied. 'I think they've decided she's the runt of the litter, and they're taking all the milk that's going.'

As they watched, the female kitten began to struggle towards her mother's teat to feed. She kept slipping, her thin legs too weak to push herself forward over her brothers' sleeping bodies. Mandy would have loved to reach in and help, but she knew this would probably upset the mother cat. It was her job to nudge the babies into place. She didn't seem too interested in her daughter at the moment, though.

Come on, you can do it! Mandy urged silently, willing the tiny creature on with all her heart. She knew how important these first few hours were, if the little kitten was going to survive.

The next morning, Mandy raced through to the residential unit as soon as she was dressed. She found her father sitting on a chair in his dressing-gown, with a dropper in one hand and a scrap of pale fur in the other. There was no need to ask which kitten he was trying to feed.

'So she's been rejected,' Mandy sighed. 'You thought that might happen, didn't you, Dad?'

Mr Hope nodded. 'I think the mother cat feels those three big males are as much as she can cope with,' he replied. 'This is her first litter, so she's quite inexperienced. This one was pushed out of the nest by her brothers last night and Mum's lost interest in her.'

'Poor thing,' Mandy said, sitting on the arm of the chair and watching as Mr Hope patiently coaxed the kitten to feed. She was mewing with a thin, reedy cry, but she hardly seemed strong enough to swallow the drops of milk. 'Do you think she's going to pull through?' Mandy asked doubtfully.

'I'm not sure,' her father answered. 'Sometimes when a mother rejects one kitten, it's because she knows there's something wrong with it. We've given her a thorough check over, though, and there aren't any obvious problems – no cleft palate to interfere with her feeding or anything like that. We'll just have to wait and see how she gets on.'

'How are the others?' Mandy asked, going over to the cage and looking in on the mother cat. She was awake and purring loudly, while the three male kittens were firmly latched on to her teats.

'They're fine,' Mr Hope said, glancing over. 'It's a case of survival of the biggest in that family, I'm afraid.'

'It seems awful they've just edged her out,'
Mandy said, looking back at the tiny female. 'She's
got as much right to live as they have.'

'Well, Mother Nature can seem cruel sometimes,' said her father, yawning. 'That's where us
vets come in handy.' He held the kitten at arm's
length and they both laughed as it sneezed a drop
of milk from the end of its bright pink nose.

'Why don't you let me take over, Dad?' Mandy
asked, quickly washing her hands. 'Looks like
you're the tired one this morning.'

'Thanks, love,' he replied, carefully handing her
the kitten. 'I don't think she's going to take any
more milk, but can you try and get her to relieve
herself before she goes back in the incubator?
There's some cotton wool here.'

Mandy held the little creature in the palm of
one hand. The kitten's ear canals were still closed,
as well as her eyes, so she couldn't hear anything.
Mandy tried to keep her movements as calm and
smooth as possible. She stroked the kitten gently
under her tail with the ball of damp cotton wool.
Normally, the mother cat would lick her babies and
encourage them to urinate and open their bowels,
but this also did the trick.

'The trouble is, I don't think the owners will be
prepared to bother with all this business,' Mr Hope

went on. 'When they came to look at the kittens yesterday afternoon, I could tell they weren't really interested in this one.'

Mandy was horrified. 'They can't abandon her too!' she said. The kitten had managed to produce a small puddle by now, so she laid her back in the warm incubator and covered her up with a blanket. 'What do they think will happen?' she asked, turning back to her father.

'I get the impression they're rather hoping she'll just fade away,' Mr Hope replied, stretching as he got up. 'They're planning on selling the kittens, and they probably think the runt of the litter won't fetch very much, even if she does pull through. I doubt they'll want to hand-rear her.'

'How can people possibly be like that?' Mandy asked, outraged. She couldn't believe anyone could be so callous. After watching Martha's life coming to its end, this new beginning seemed even more precious to her than ever. She knew that the odds were stacked against this little kitten – hand-reared animals often didn't survive – but she was determined to do everything she could to help her. In a strange kind of way, she felt as though she owed it to Martha.

Six

'How's the kitten?' Mandy asked her mother anxiously, as soon as she and James arrived back at Animal Ark that afternoon. 'James has come back to have a look at her too. We called in at his house on the way, so his mum knows all about it.'

'Good,' her mother smiled, sipping a mug of tea. 'And as for our little reject – Simon's been feeding her every hour or so and she seems to have taken to the bottle quite well.'

'That's great!' Mandy beamed, taking off her schoolbag. 'I've been worrying about her all day.'

'Just remember, though, it's still early days,' her mother warned. 'You know how quickly things can go wrong with newborns. And we've got no idea what's going to happen to her over the next week or so. There don't seem to be any nursing cats near by who might be able to foster her, I'm afraid.'

'Is it worth talking to the owners again?' James asked. 'Won't they change their minds about hand-rearing the kitten if she seems to be doing better?'

Mrs Hope shook her head. 'They've definitely decided against it,' she said. 'You should have seen their faces when I said she'd need feeding at least every two hours through the night! I told them how rewarding it could be, but they were horrified at the very thought.'

'They don't know what they're missing!' Mandy said. 'How can they turn down the chance to save her life? It's the most fantastic thing they could ever do.' She turned to James. 'Do you remember when we looked after Delilah's kittens? It was great, wasn't it?'

Delilah was a Persian cat who'd been injured on the road when her kittens were only a few weeks old, so James and Mandy had helped rear them during their half-term holiday. It had been hard work, but wonderful to see the tiny animals growing stronger every day.

'It was a struggle to get them to take the bottle at first,' James reminded her. 'They were much happier when Blossom took them in, weren't they?' Blossom was a stray tabby who'd just had kittens of her own and managed to feed Delilah's too.

'Yes, and they'd already had Delilah's milk for a few weeks, which gave them a good start,' Mrs Hope said. 'Their chances were a lot better than our little reject.' Noticing Mandy's worried expression, she added more cheerfully, 'Still, at least she's feeding well now, and she seems quite comfortable in the incubator.'

'And we'll give her all the love and care she needs, seeing as the Brewers can't be bothered!' Mandy declared. 'James and I could look after her at night, if Simon can carry on feeding her in the day. We'll take it in turns—'

'Now, Mandy, that's just impossible and you know it,' Mrs Hope broke in firmly. 'You two couldn't be up all night in the middle of term! You've been looking tired enough recently as it is. No, if anyone's going to feed her at night, it'll be your father or me. For the time being, anyway.'

Mandy opened her mouth to argue, but one look from her mum made her close it again. 'Well, at least we can do something now,' she said, turning to leave. 'Come on, James – let's go through to the unit.'

'Fine,' Mrs Hope replied, rinsing her mug in the sink. 'The Brewers are coming to take the mother and her male kittens home tomorrow, so you might as well enjoy them now. Oh, and Geraldine's coming in to afternoon surgery in half an hour or so,' she added, wiping her hands on a tea towel. 'Have you finished with those books you borrowed?'

'Not quite,' Mandy said, pausing by the kitchen door. 'I hope everything's OK with her. Do you know why she made the appointment?'

Mrs Hope shook her head. 'She didn't mention anything to Jean on the phone,' she said, gathering her long red hair into a ponytail.

'Maybe she wants to talk about what was wrong with Martha,' James suggested, following Mandy out of the room. 'Sometimes it's difficult to take things in when you're upset.'

'Could be,' Mandy agreed. James often managed to put his finger on the way people were feeling. 'Let's try and catch her later, after we've had a look at the kittens.'

'She's beautiful, isn't she?' James said, looking at the Burmese as she lay contentedly licking one of her litter. Like Mandy, he didn't risk upsetting her by picking any of the kittens up, but just watched them through the wire of the cage. Two of them were feeding, their tiny legs tangled together. The mother cat had scooped the third between her

front paws and was giving him a thorough wash.

'I love Burmese cats,' Simon said, glancing over. He finished topping up the food bowl of a sleepy-looking rat who was curled up in a nest of shredded paper, and came over to stand beside James. 'They're so elegant, but they'll play with you for hours – just like a dog.'

'I'm sure this little one's going to be as gorgeous as her mother,' Mandy said, softly stroking the female kitten's head as she lay in the incubator. She still looked very fragile, but at least it seemed she was feeding well now. It would only be the warmth and companionship of her family that she missed.

'How can you tell?' James asked. 'I think they only begin to look sweet once their eyes have opened.'

'I just know,' Mandy said quietly. 'There's something special about her – I can feel it.' Seeing the smallest kitten all alone, while her brothers were getting so much attention from their mother, had really touched her heart.

The kitten had begun to mew and was trying to lift her wobbly head. It looked as though she was getting hungry, so Mandy put on her white coat and began to wash her hands in case she was needed.

'I'd better start getting ready for surgery,' Simon said, looking at his watch. 'Can I leave you two in charge for the moment? The rat should be fine – just coming round from his anaesthetic – but Kitty's due for a feed about now.'

'Sure,' Mandy replied, reaching for the powdered milk. 'Right, James – let's see if we've still got that magic touch with the bottle!'

Mandy and James were on their way back from the unit, feeling very pleased with themselves for having managed to give the kitten a good feed, when they found Geraldine and Robbie sitting in the waiting-room.

'Hi there, Robbie,' Mandy said cheerfully, giving the beagle a pat. 'Hey, what's the matter? You don't look very happy.'

Instead of leaping all around her, Robbie merely raised his head and pushed it against Mandy's hand. He didn't get to his feet, even when James clicked his fingers and whistled.

'He isn't, I'm afraid,' said Geraldine with a wan smile. 'That's why we're here. I'm really worried about him!'

'Well, I suppose he's bound to be upset for a while,' Mandy replied, settling on the chair next to them. 'He'll be missing Martha too, won't he? Just like you.' Geraldine looked as though she hadn't slept properly for days, and her eyes were red-rimmed.

'I know,' Geraldine said anxiously, 'but I've got this awful feeling it might be more than that.' She put a hand under Robbie's chin and lifted his head, looking into his deep, sad eyes. 'All he wants to do is lie in the basket all day, cuddled up to Mouse – exactly like Martha did when she was so ill.'

'It's only been a couple of days, though, hasn't it? Since you lost her, I mean,' James said, stroking Robbie's ear. 'He'll probably be back to normal soon.'

'No, you don't understand!' Geraldine said, her voice rising as she became more agitated. 'He doesn't want to go outside and he won't eat, either. And you know how he normally loves his food. I think there's something seriously wrong with Robbie! What if he's caught what Martha had?'

Mandy looked at James, not quite sure how to reply. If Robbie hadn't been eating, it sounded as though he might well be ill. At the very least, he must be quite weak by now, and he wasn't a young dog any more. No wonder Geraldine was worried. Luckily, at that moment Mrs Hope put her head round the door to call Geraldine through to the surgery.

'I'm sure Mum can put your mind at rest,' Mandy said, helping to coax Robbie up from the floor. He really didn't want to go anywhere, but with Geraldine pulling from the front and James and Mandy pushing from behind, they eventually managed to get him into the treatment room. Simon lifted him up on to the table, and he stood there with his head down and tail drooping.

'We'll wait outside for you,' Mandy promised Geraldine. The room felt quite crowded with so many people in it. 'Shall we go and see if Jean needs a hand in reception?' she suggested to James.

'I hope Robbie's going to be OK,' he said, after he'd closed the door behind them. 'He does look miserable, doesn't he?'

Mandy just shook her head. She couldn't bear to see the beagle so upset. 'Come on, perhaps there's some filing we can do,' she sighed. 'A really boring job might take our mind off things.'

A little while later, they had just pulled out the notes for an accident-prone hamster called Lucky, when Geraldine appeared in the reception area again. Robbie trailed dejectedly behind her, a look in his eyes which seemed to say, *When will this be over?*

'Well?' Mandy asked anxiously, coming out from behind the desk. 'What did Mum think? Did she find anything?'

'Nothing obvious,' Geraldine replied. 'She's taken a blood sample to see if his kidneys and liver are working OK, but everything seems to be normal. Apart from his lack of appetite, that is, and the lethargy.'

James had walked over to join them. 'But surely it would be unlikely for Robbie to have caught anything from Martha, wouldn't it?' he asked, frowning behind his glasses.

'That's right,' Mandy agreed. 'Mum told me that viruses hardly ever pass from one species of animal to another. And FIV isn't highly contagious, anyway.'

Geraldine ran one hand through her dark curly hair. 'I know it sounds crazy,' she said in a rush, 'but I just can't get the idea out of my head that he's got that horrible disease too. He seems to have the same symptoms as Martha. When I look at him lying there in the basket. . .' She shook her head, unable to carry on.

'Honestly, Geraldine, that's so unlikely,' Mandy said positively, trying to convince her. 'When Mum's tested Robbie's blood, I'm sure it'll turn out to be quite clear. Then you'll know for certain.'

'That's true,' Geraldine said. 'And I suppose it won't be too long to wait. I'm bringing him back at the beginning of surgery tomorrow.' She bent down to hug Robbie tightly and added, 'I just couldn't bear to lose him, too – not so soon after saying goodbye to Martha. I really think it would break my heart.'

'I'm sure that's not going to happen,' Mandy said gently. She could see Geraldine was close to tears, and caught James's eye. Was there anything they could say that might cheer her up?

'Have you shown Geraldine your project yet, Mandy?' he asked, getting the idea straight away. 'I bet she'd like to see how it's coming on.'

'Good idea!' Mandy replied, flashing him a grateful smile. 'Why don't we go through to the cottage? If you've got time, that is, Geraldine?'

'Of course,' she said, summoning up a smile. 'Let me just make this appointment and then I'm all yours. I'm sorry! I've been so wrapped up in my own problems I haven't even asked how you've been getting on.'

'I'm really glad I chose this subject,' Mandy said, when Geraldine had fixed everything up with Jean and the three of them were walking through to the house with Robbie. 'It was James's brilliant idea, you know.' And she patted him on the back.

James immediately started blushing, so Mandy went on quickly, 'I've just started writing about all the different jobs the worker bees do. You know, looking after the queen and the grubs to begin with, and then making wax, and guarding the hive, and collecting pollen and nectar. There's so much to say!'

'This is wonderful,' Geraldine said as she sat at the kitchen table and looked over Mandy's work, clipped into a loose-leaf file. Robbie had padded over to the Aga and slumped against it with a sigh. 'You've managed to fit in so much interesting information. Your teacher should be delighted.'

'Huh!' Mandy snorted. 'I'm not so sure about

that. He's looking at my plan for the whole thing at the moment, but I bet he'll find some fault with it. Nothing I do is ever good enough for him!'

'Oh, come on,' James protested, looking over Geraldine's shoulder at a page of illustrations. 'He'll have to admit you've really worked hard on this. Your diagrams are amazing! They must have taken you ages.'

'They did,' Mandy said. 'I hardly noticed the time going by, though. You don't when you're really interested in something, do you?'

'No,' Geraldine agreed, gazing up from the file with a wistful expression. She sighed. 'I think that's why I feel so low at the moment – not enough to think about. Bees are fascinating, but I've learned all about them now. I need to get stuck into some-thing new to take my mind off things.' She stretched her arms with a yawn and added, 'I've been thinking about getting some day-old chicks to rear. There's an incubator in the outhouse, after all – might as well put it to good use.'

Mandy froze. She felt like a character in a car-toon, with a flashing light bulb over her head, and she could see that the very same thought had struck James. Of course! Why had it taken them so long to realise? Geraldine was the ideal person to rear their kitten. She'd know exactly what to do.

After all, she'd taken on Robbie when he'd been abandoned by his mother, hadn't she? And if everything went well, having a new pet to love might help her get over losing Martha.

'D'you know, I've just had a great idea . . .' Mandy began cautiously, choosing her words carefully. Geraldine *had* to agree to look after the little Burmese. It would be the perfect solution!

Seven

'No, I'm sorry, Mandy,' Geraldine said firmly, pushing back her chair from the table. 'There's no way I could rear your kitten. I couldn't possibly take on such a big commitment just now!'

'But isn't it exactly what you were looking for?' Mandy asked desperately. 'You said you needed something else to think about, didn't you? And she's such a dear little thing!'

'It would be wonderful to know you were taking care of her,' James added hopefully. 'I'm sure she couldn't have a better home anywhere.'

'Chicks are one thing – a newborn kitten is quite another,' Geraldine declared, pushing her hands into the pockets of her jacket. She looked at their eager faces and her voice softened a little. 'You know how much I'd love to help, but I've got Robbie to think about too,' she went on. 'Even if he doesn't have FIV, what if the blood test shows he has some other disease? The kitten could easily pick up an infection.'

'She wouldn't catch anything from Robbie, though,' Mandy replied. She jumped up and started to fill the kettle. If they could keep Geraldine here for a cup of tea, they'd surely be able to talk her round. 'It's not as though they're the same species. If he *is* ill, you only need to worry about keeping him away from other dogs.'

'Well, you know what I think about that,' Geraldine replied. 'I still feel as though Robbie did catch something from Martha, despite what everyone says.' She closed the file and pushed it back across the table.

'Besides,' she went on tiredly, 'it's just too soon. I had Martha for fourteen years and it's only been a few days since she died. I need time to get over losing her. Robbie does, too. He doesn't want a little kitten rushing around and teasing him to death.'

They all looked over to where the beagle was lying, curled in a dejected heap against the Aga. 'Poor boy,' Mandy said, going over to stroke his smooth coat. 'You need something to cheer you up, don't you?'

Robbie licked her hand a couple of times, then rested his head back on his paws. He glanced up at her, almost timidly. The furrow between his eyes seemed deeper than ever, and now he looked as though he was frowning unhappily.

'All the bounce has gone out of him, hasn't it?' Geraldine said, standing beside Mandy. 'Come on, old thing,' she went on, encouraging Robbie to get up. 'Time to go home. There's some calf's-foot jelly in the fridge, just for you.'

'Won't you stay for some tea?' Mandy asked, playing for time.

'Or why not come through to the unit and just take a look at the kitten?' James added. 'Mandy thinks she's going to grow into the most beautiful cat.'

'You two don't give up easily, do you?' Geraldine teased. She went on more seriously, 'Look, I'm sure your kitten's gorgeous, and you won't have any trouble finding someone to bring her up. But it won't be me, I'm afraid. You're just going to have to accept that. OK?'

'OK,' James agreed reluctantly, and Mandy eventually nodded too.

For now, she added privately to herself. At least

she'd put the idea into Geraldine's head. Maybe if she thought it over for a few days, she'd change her mind. Mandy could just imagine the kitten in a few months' time, chasing butterflies across the lawn at Wood Vale. She'd be so happy there, and she'd make them so happy too! Surely Geraldine would realise that sooner or later?

The next day, Mandy and James were chatting in the corridor at the end of afternoon school when Mr Marsh came hurrying towards them.

'Ah, Amanda!' he said. 'Just the person! Can I have a quick word?'

Mandy's face must have given away her feelings, because he smiled and added, 'There's nothing to worry about. I only want to talk to you about the plan you handed in yesterday, that's all.'

'Oh! Fine,' Mandy said, still rather suspicious. She steeled herself for whatever he might say next and asked, 'Do you think it's all right?'

'Better than all right,' Mr Marsh replied as he searched through his briefcase. 'This outline is excellent! You've found out a lot about your subject already, and I can see how interested you are in it. If you can keep up this standard of work, your project will be very good indeed. Here we are.' He pulled the sheet of paper out of his case

and gave it back to her. 'I've scribbled a few com-
ments in the margin, but they're only sugges-
tions,' he added. 'Well done! I always knew you
could do it.'

'Thank you, sir,' Mandy said as she took the
sheet, still pinching herself inside. She'd never
seen Mr Marsh look so friendly. He was positively
beaming at her!

'Not at all,' he replied, already starting off again
towards the staffroom. Then he turned and called
back, 'I'm taking the detention class this week. We
could go over your project together then, if you
like. You'll be bringing it in for Friday's lesson,
won't you?'

'Yes, Mr Marsh,' Mandy said faintly. 'That would
be great! Thanks.'

She and James stared at each other when Mr
Marsh had gone. 'I thought you said he'd got it in
for you?' James said.

'It's like he's changed into a different person,'
Mandy replied slowly. 'He was really nice then,
wasn't he? I kept waiting for him to say something
horrible and he never did.'

'Just so long as he doesn't change back again by
Friday,' James said. 'Let's go home! I've had
enough of school for one day. Can I come back
with you and see how the kitten's doing? I told

Mum I'd probably go to your house again today.'

'Perhaps you should just move in,' Mandy teased, walking off with him down the corridor.

She took a deep breath as they went out into the open air, lifting her face up to the sun. A sudden rush of happiness seemed to fill her body. There had been so much to worry about recently: first Martha, then the rejected kitten, and Robbie being so depressed. Friday's detention had been lurking in the back of her mind too, casting a shadow over everything. Now, after that quick conversation with Mr Marsh, she felt full of hope and energy again. She was determined to do whatever she could to help Geraldine get Robbie back on his feet. And she'd find someone to look after the little Burmese, too.

'Let's get a move on,' she called to James as she started sprinting towards the bike rack. 'We've got places to go, and people to see!'

When Mandy and James arrived back at Animal Ark, they found Mrs Hope in the residential unit. She was keeping an eye on the Burmese and her kittens, while she finished writing up their notes.

'You're just in time to say goodbye to this little family,' she told the two friends with a smile. 'We're expecting the Brewers to come and collect them any minute.'

'They look very settled now, don't they?' Mandy commented. One of the kittens was feeding steadily while the other two slept.

'Yes, I'm glad the mother's managed to bond with those three, at least,' Mrs Hope said, laying down her pen.

James was peering into the incubator, where the female kitten lay snuggled under her blanket. 'She's so tiny, isn't she?' he breathed.

'She's bigger than she was,' Mandy said, coming to stand beside him. 'I think she's growing every day.' She knew how quickly things could go wrong with hand-reared puppies and kittens – they often just faded away without any warning. So far, though, this little female looked like a fighter.

Then she turned to her mother, remembering the other problem on her mind. 'Have you had a look at Robbie's blood yet, Mum?' she asked. 'Is everything OK?'

'Well, there's no sign of infection,' her mother replied. 'He's slightly anaemic, but probably only because he hasn't been eating properly. There's no way he could have caught FIV from Martha, but at least now we can convince Geraldine.'

'Say Geraldine was to get another cat quite soon – or maybe even a kitten – could the virus could be passed on somehow?' Mandy asked her mother innocently.

Mrs Hope shook her head. 'No, that would be very unlikely,' she said. 'It might be a good idea to wash Martha's bedding and disinfect her food bowl, but only as a precaution.' She shot Mandy a searching glance and added, 'Why do you ask, love? Geraldine hasn't said anything about getting another cat, has she? I'd have thought it was rather soon for that.'

'Oh, no reason in particular,' Mandy replied vaguely. 'Just thinking ahead.' She shot James a warning look, in case he was about to give their plan away. She knew her mother would tell her to let Geraldine choose a new pet in her own good time. The trouble was, her own good time would be too late for their kitten.

'I know that expression on your face,' Mrs Hope said, narrowing her green eyes. 'You're planning something, aren't you?'

Before she could say any more, though, Simon put his head round the door and announced, 'Mr and Mrs Brewer are in the waiting-room. Are you ready for me to show them through? They've brought a big laundry hamper so we can put the kittening box straight in.'

'That's a good idea,' Mrs Hope said approvingly.

'Yes, bring them in. I know they can't wait to get Persephone home.'

'Persephone?' Mandy repeated. 'That's a very fancy name. I wonder what they're going to call the kittens!'

'Why don't we give this little female a name?' James asked. 'If she's going to stay here for a while, we might as well.'

'I'm not sure,' Mandy said, gazing at the tiny, helpless creature. 'Don't you think we should leave that up to whoever looks after her? I'm trying not to get any more attached to her than I am already.'

'She is adorable, isn't she?' her mother said. 'I must say, I don't know how the Brewers can resist her.'

Just at that moment, the door opened and Simon showed the Brewers through.

'And how's my darling Persephone?' Mrs Brewer cooed, rushing straight over to her cat without glancing at anyone else. 'How's my clever girl and her dear little kitties?'

She was smartly dressed, with a swirly silk scarf knotted over her large bosom, and she smelled strongly of some overpowering perfume. There was something about her that Mandy didn't particularly like, and she could tell from James's expression that he felt the same.

'So these are your helpers?' Mr Brewer said to Mandy's mum, nodding at James and Mandy. He was a short, stout man, dressed in a navy blazer with shiny gilt buttons. 'Well, you've done a fine job between you. Three handsome kittens for us to take home, and we've already got a queue of buyers anxious to see them.'

'Bring them back for their first vaccinations in about eight weeks' time, won't you?' Mrs Hope said. 'And I'll give you a diet sheet to help keep Persephone's strength up.'

Simon carefully loaded the box carrying the Burmese and her kittens into the laundry basket, and Mrs Brewer put a blanket over the top. 'That'll help her feel more secure,' she said. 'We have to take care of our precious girl, don't we?'

She glanced quickly over to the incubator and added, 'It's a shame about the female, but I really don't think we could manage her as well as these three. Besides, she won't be a good mother herself if she's been hand-reared. We couldn't sell her for much.'

'We're still looking for someone who's willing to look after her,' Mrs Hope said, opening the door through to the surgery. 'We'll let you know what happens.'

'Tell you what,' Mr Brewer said, squaring his

shoulders. 'If anyone manages to raise that kitten, they can keep her. We won't expect to be paid a penny, either. Someone might end up with quite a bargain on their hands!'

'Oh, Nigel! You're too soft for your own good,' Mrs Brewer said, sailing out and leaving Simon to carry the basket. 'Now come on, let's put Persephone and her babies in the Range Rover.'

Mandy followed them, fuming inwardly. She couldn't understand how the Brewers could just leave the female kitten behind without a second thought. Didn't they feel any sense of responsibility towards her? All they seemed to think about was money!

'Oh, do be careful!' Mrs Brewer told Simon, as he took the basket through the reception area. 'There's a dog! Keep Persephone well away, please.'

Geraldine was sitting there with Robbie at her feet, flicking through a magazine as she waited for their appointment. Mrs Brewer needn't have worried, though. Robbie didn't show any interest in the cats at all – he didn't even raise his head as they were carried past.

Mandy and James said hello to Geraldine and made a big fuss of Robbie, while Simon and the Brewers settled Persephone into their big, gleaming car.

'That's the Burmese I was telling you about,'
Mandy said to Geraldine, watching them through the
open doorway. 'Her owners are taking her home
now, with the three male kittens.'

She racked her brains to think of something to
say that might change Geraldine's mind about
rearing the female kitten. This was the ideal oppor-

tunity! When the Brewers came back to settle up their bill, she decided to seize her moment. Perhaps if Geraldine saw what they were like, she'd take pity on the little Burmese.

'Excuse me, Mrs Brewer,' she began, as politely as she could manage. 'Are you sure you're not going to have second thoughts about leaving the female kitten behind? My parents think she's got a good chance of surviving.'

'She may well *survive*, dear,' Mrs Brewer replied, turning round from the desk and looking down her nose at Mandy, 'but that's not really the point, is it? We won't be able to breed from her and I can't imagine anyone wanting to buy her – especially not after they've heard that she was rejected. She's really not much use to anyone.'

Geraldine was listening to every word of this, and a flush began to creep over her pale cheeks. Mandy could tell, from one quick glance, that she was beginning to rise to the bait.

'I bet that little one would make a lovely pet, though,' she went on. 'Wouldn't you like to keep her for yourselves?'

'Listen, dear,' Mrs Brewer said firmly. 'We've got enough to do, looking after these healthy kittens and their mother. We could spend all our time trying to raise this sickly one and there's no saying how she'd turn out in the end. If you can find someone prepared to take the risk, then fine. But frankly, it's not worth our while. She's the runt of the litter, and I'm afraid she's never going to amount to very much.'

This was too much for Geraldine. She rose to her feet and said pleasantly, 'Excuse me for inter-rupting, but don't you think you might be speaking too soon? My dog here was the runt of the litter, and look at him now!'

'Doesn't that prove my point?' Mrs Brewer said, glancing down at Robbie. He lifted his sad eyes up to meet hers, and then tried to curl himself into an even tighter ball under Geraldine's chair. 'I'm sure you're very fond of him, but he is rather a miser-able-looking specimen, isn't he?' she went on. 'It might have been kinder to let nature take its course.'

She took her husband's arm. 'Now, Nigel, if we've paid our dues then we should be off. Mustn't keep Persephone waiting.'

'What a terrible woman!' Geraldine exploded when the Brewers had gone. 'How can she talk like that?' She crouched down and hugged Robbie tightly, muttering, '"Miserable-looking specimen", indeed! Well, I'll show her. I've a good mind to—'

'Yes?' Mandy said eagerly, as Geraldine and

Robbie followed Mrs Hope through to the surgery for their appointment. 'A good mind to what?'

'Wait 'til I've had a word with your mother,' Geraldine replied over her shoulder. 'You'll see.'

'What was that all about?' James asked Mandy curiously, when they were alone. 'Why did you try and make Mrs Brewer keep the other kitten? You must have known she didn't want to.'

'I wanted to show Geraldine what she was like, that's all,' Mandy replied. 'I thought listening to Mrs Brewer would put Geraldine on our side and make her feel like looking after the kitten. And, James – I think I might have succeeded!'

Eight

Mandy pottered about in the residential unit, sweeping the floor and tidying up, with one ear open for the sound of footsteps in the corridor. James had gone home to take Blackie for a walk, but she wanted to stay around to find out whether her plan had been successful. Was Geraldine going to offer to rear the kitten herself? If so, she'd be bound to come in and have a look at her. She'd almost given up hope when Simon appeared beside her, grinning broadly.

'Problem solved!' he said, waving an arm towards Geraldine, who was following close behind. 'Here's our guardian angel.'

'I wouldn't go as far as that,' Geraldine smiled.

'But I have changed my mind about looking after your kitten, Mandy. The way that dreadful woman just wrote her off! It made my blood boil.'

'That's wonderful!' Mandy said, beaming too. 'Oh, I knew all along you'd be the perfect person to rear her.' She led Geraldine over to the incubator and told her proudly, 'Look, there's Kitty. Isn't she lovely?'

'She looks so lonely, though, all on her own in there,' Geraldine said quietly. 'Poor little thing. I think she's going to need a lot of help.'

As they watched, the kitten lifted her head and gave a weak mew. She tried to move forward across the soft blanket, but her legs weren't yet strong enough to support her and she could only wave them helplessly.

'Looks like she's hungry again,' Simon said. 'Would you like to feed her, Geraldine? Might as well get stuck in straight away.'

'Where's Robbie?' Mandy asked, noticing for the first time that Geraldine was on her own. 'Everything's OK, isn't it?'

'As far as we can tell,' Geraldine replied. 'Don't worry, he's safely in the car. Your mother tells me his blood's clear, and there's no danger of him passing anything on to this little one. But if you don't mind, Simon, I'd better take him home now.

Can you carry on looking after the kitten here 'til Friday? That'll give me a day to get everything ready, and I can collect her on Friday morning.'

'Sure,' Simon said. 'As for her next feed – I have to go back into the surgery now, but perhaps our willing assistant can take over?' And he raised his eyebrows at Mandy.

'I'd love to,' she replied. 'After all, if the kitten's not going to be here for much longer, I'd better make the most of her.'

'You'll come and visit, though, won't you, Mandy?' Geraldine asked, taking a last look at the kitten before she turned to leave. 'I'll have my hands full, what with spoon-feeding Robbie and bottle-feeding this little one. Any offers of help will be gratefully received!'

'Of course,' Mandy assured her. 'There's nothing I'd like more, and I bet James feels the same. I'll ring him in a minute. Shall we come over on Saturday?'

'That would be perfect,' Geraldine said, giving her a quick hug. 'Well, this might turn out to be a mistake, but there's no going back now. And d'you know, I feel better already. This little kitten's going to be a beauty, and that snooty woman will have to eat her words.'

'She will,' Mandy echoed. 'And we'll get Robbie

back to his old self, too. Just you wait and see, Geraldine. Everything's going to be fine!'

Mandy left enough time for James to come back from his walk, and then phoned to tell him the good news about Geraldine looking after the kitten. He was delighted, and Mandy felt even more sure that all their problems would soon be sorted out. She was almost looking forward to Friday's biology lesson!

But when Friday morning came, though, it was soon clear that Mr Marsh's good mood had come and gone. He wasn't irritable, exactly, but his mind seemed to be on other things. If anyone had a question to ask him, they had to repeat it several times before getting an answer. His wavy brown hair looked more untidy than usual, and when he sat down at the desk, Mandy noticed he was wearing odd socks.

'I wonder what's up with him?' Vicki Simpson whispered. Mandy just shrugged her shoulders. She didn't want to risk getting in to any more trouble – one detention was enough for anybody.

As soon as the bell went at the end of their lesson, Mr Marsh rushed out of the room. Mandy wouldn't have been surprised if he'd forgotten all about taking the detention class. But at the end of the afternoon, there he was, waiting for her to arrive.

'Good! I'm glad you're here, Amanda,' he said. 'I see from the list that it's only the two of us today. Now I just have to nip out to my car, so get on with your work for the moment, please. You've brought something to do, haven't you?'

'Yes, Mr Marsh,' Mandy said, slightly surprised. 'I've brought my project. You said you'd go through it with me, remember?'

'Oh, so I did,' he replied. 'That's right. You're studying bats, aren't you? Very interesting.'

'Well, actually I'm writing about bees,' Mandy said, sitting down at one of the desks in the empty classroom and taking out her books. She couldn't believe Mr Marsh had already forgotten what her project was about, especially after giving her such a glowing report on the outline.

'Of course, bees,' Mr Marsh said, jingling some change in his pockets as he shifted from one leg to the other. 'Yes, it's all coming back to me now. Right, well, I'll be back in a second.' And with that he dashed off again, jumpy as a cat on a windy day.

Mandy began to read over what she'd written so far. She was about to begin describing how bees turned the nectar they'd collected into honey. The books Geraldine had lent her didn't explain the process very clearly, though. Mandy knew the bees stored pollen in baskets on their back legs. But where did they keep the nectar? And what did they do with it once they were back at the hive? She gazed out of the window, racking her brains to try to remember what Geraldine had said.

Then suddenly she caught sight of Mr Marsh down below, fiddling about with something in his car. What could he be up to? He was sitting on one of the back seats, next to what looked like a large wire-mesh cage. Mandy stood up to get a better view, her curiosity aroused at once. Did he have some kind of animal in there? Just at that moment, though, Mr Marsh glanced up towards the classroom window, so she quickly sat down again. By the time he was back in the room, five minutes later, she was reading her textbook intently.

'Fine! Working hard, I see. Well done,' he said vaguely, rubbing his hands as he sat down at the desk and took a book out of his briefcase. 'Let me know if you have any problems.'

So much for going through my project together, Mandy thought to herself. She looked over at Mr Marsh, wondering if she could interrupt him with a question. Then she gasped out loud. A small, white, furry head was peeping inquisitively out of his jacket pocket.

'Is anything wrong?' Mr Marsh asked, looking up. Wordlessly, Mandy pointed towards his jacket, and his eyes travelled downwards in the direction of her finger.

'Oh,' he sighed, laying down his book. 'Looks like I'll have to come clean. You've found me out, Amanda!'

Mandy began to giggle as a second, darker head popped out of the other pocket. 'I didn't know you kept rats, Mr Marsh!' she exclaimed. 'They're beautiful!'

'Well, I think so,' he replied, taking one of the rats out of his pocket and stroking its head affectionately. 'But you'd be surprised how many people scream at the sight of them. Here, do you want to take a closer look?'

'Yes please,' Mandy said eagerly, walking up to the teacher's desk. 'I love rats – they're so intelligent and friendly, aren't they? We often treat them at the surgery, and one of my friends has got pet rats.'

'Oh yes, I remember Miss Temple telling me your parents were vets,' Mr Marsh said. 'Well, this is Eenie,' he went on, putting the white rat into Mandy's hands. 'And here's her friend Meenie. They're both female.' He scooped the second animal out of his pocket and held her up. She was white too, but with a dark grey head and intelligent, black eyes. 'Not very original names, I'm afraid.'

Mandy held Eenie securely against her body and looked down into the rat's beady pink eyes. Her delicate ears were shell-pink too, but the rest of her body was pure white, from the tips of her whiskers to the end of her smooth, curving tail. Eenie stretched her twitching nose forward, sniffed Mandy delicately and then climbed up to her shoulder. There she settled comfortably, lying around Mandy's neck like a warm furry scarf and snuffling into her ear.

'I can tell this is Eenie's favourite place,' Mandy said, laughing at the tickly sensation. 'She's wheezing a bit, though, isn't she?' She'd noticed the rat was making a rattling sound as she breathed.

Mr Marsh frowned, putting Meenie down on the desk and scratching her gently behind the ears. 'This one's been sneezing and snuffling, too,' he said. 'Listen, you can hear her now. I'm worried about the pair of them – that's why I brought them in to school with me today. I didn't want to leave them on their own for too long. I put their cage in the back of my car, and I've been rushing out between lessons to see if they're OK.'

'I'm sure you could have brought them into the lab,' Mandy said. 'The headmaster wouldn't have minded.' She took Eenie down from her neck and examined her more closely, adding, 'Miss Temple used to keep a hamster as a school pet, you know.'

'Well, I didn't want to ask,' Mr Marsh said. 'I thought it might have put you all off your work. I've found it pretty distracting having them around, I must admit.'

'They're nice and lively, aren't they?' Mandy observed, as Meenie wriggled her way up the sleeve of Mr Marsh's jacket and popped her head out at his shoulder. 'Are they eating normally?'

'From what I can tell,' Mr Marsh replied. 'Apart from the wheezing and sneezing, they seem to be fine.'

Mandy thought hard. 'Has anything changed in their routine recently?' she asked Mr Marsh. 'You haven't started them on any new kind of food, by any chance?'

Mr Marsh shook his head. 'Not that I can think of,' he said. 'Why do you ask?'

'Well, they might have developed an allergy to something,' Mandy replied, cradling Eenie in the crook of her arm and stroking the back of the rat's head. 'Either that, or it's some sort of respiratory infection. Can you take them to a vet fairly soon for a check-up?'

'I'm going to make an appointment as soon as I get home,' Mr Marsh said anxiously, letting Meenie run from one of his hands to the other. 'It's just so difficult to fit these things in when you're out at work all day.'

He gazed out of the window and then suddenly jumped to his feet, tucking Meenie back in his jacket pocket. 'Come on!' he said, taking Eenie from Mandy's hands. 'It's a beautiful sunny afternoon, and the weekend's nearly here. Why don't I declare this detention officially over? After all, I gave it to you. Now I'm going to take it back!'

'Are you sure?' Mandy said uncertainly, unable to believe her luck. It was hard to know where she was, with Mr Marsh changing like this all the time. And then she had a brilliant idea.

'Why don't you come home with me now?' she said to him. 'Afternoon surgery will be starting any minute. I'm sure Mum or Dad could have a quick look at Eenie and Meenie for you.'

'Do you think they'd mind?' Mr Marsh asked, letting Eenie ride on his shoulder. 'It would be a great relief to me, that's for sure.'

'Oh, the only trouble is, I've got my bike with me,' Mandy said, as she began to pack away her books. Her face fell. 'It won't fit in your car, will it?'

'No, but we can put it on the back. I've got a special rack for my own bike,' Mr Marsh replied, putting Eenie safely in the other pocket and picking up his briefcase. 'That's one problem with an easy solution.'

Ten minutes later, Mandy's bike was safely strapped to Mr Marsh's car, Eenie and Meenie were back in their cage, and they were all setting off for Animal Ark. Mandy fastened her safety belt, taking a look round the car. It was a real mess! Books and papers were lying everywhere, spilling out of Mr Marsh's briefcase on the back seat and scattered over the floor by her feet. The air was beautifully fragrant, though. She took a deep breath, wondering if he used some kind of air freshener.

'The rats' cage smells great, doesn't it?' Mr Marsh commented. 'I've bought these wonderful cedarwood shavings from the pet shop for Eenie and Meenie's bedding. They must feel like they're sleeping out in a forest.'

'What?' Mandy almost squeaked in her excitement. 'How long ago was this?'

'Oh, a couple of days,' Mr Marsh replied. 'Why do you ask?'

'Well, I bet that's it!' Mandy exclaimed. 'Shavings can cause rats all sorts of problems, particularly cedar. It's the oils in the wood, you see – irritating their airways.'

'D'you know, I think you've hit on something there,' Mr Marsh said slowly. 'The rats have been wheezing ever since I changed their litter. Why didn't I think of that before?'

'Well, sounds like it could be the answer,' Mandy said, happy to think she might have solved the problem. 'Still, it might be a good idea to get them checked over – just to make doubly sure.'

'Thanks, Amanda,' Mr Marsh said, flashing her a smile. 'If we can get Eenie and Meenie back to normal, it'll be a big weight off my mind.'

They drove along quietly for a few minutes and then he added, rather awkwardly, 'You probably feel I've been a bit hard on you lately, what with this detention and everything.'

'Oh, that's all right,' Mandy said, wondering what was coming next.

'The thing is, I think you could do really well in biology,' he went on. 'Miss Temple told me what a keen student you were, but you seemed to have switched off in my lessons. I wanted to get you back on track, that's all. When you seemed to be work-ing so hard on your project, I was delighted. Of course it was about bees – how could I have for-gotten that?'

'Sometimes I do find it hard to think about one thing at a time,' Mandy admitted. 'And there's been a lot going on at home recently.'

Mr Marsh was so much easier to talk to, out of school, that before Mandy knew it, she'd begun to tell him all about Geraldine and her bees, and then the whole story of Martha and Robbie came spilling out.

'My parents had a beagle when I was growing up,' Mr Marsh said. 'They're wonderful dogs – really affectionate and lively. Bouncer used to wait by our gate for me to come home from school every day. I was heartbroken when he died. There probably wasn't anything we could have done, but all the same. . .' And he shook his head sadly.

Mandy felt a pang of guilt as she remembered Robbie. She'd been so taken up with the kitten these last few days, when maybe she should have been concentrating on him. She'd last seen him a couple of days ago, and she hadn't even rung Geraldine since then to find out how he was. Still, she and James were going to Wood Vale tomorrow. She'd spend lots of time with him – as long as it took to tempt his appetite back.

'What happened to Bouncer?' she asked Mr Marsh, not certain whether she really wanted to hear the answer.

'He picked up some infection or other,' he replied. 'By the time we got him to the vet, his kidneys had been damaged and he had to be put to sleep a few days later.' He gave a sad smile. 'We should have realised something was seriously wrong when he stopped eating. Beagles certainly love their food!'

Mandy stared out of the car window, trying not to let herself panic. She told herself that if Robbie did have a similar problem, her mother would certainly have picked it up straight away. She was too good a vet to miss any warning signs and, besides, she'd tested Robbie's blood. But Mr Marsh's words echoed over and over in Mandy's head: 'Something seriously wrong. . . stopped eating. . .'

What *was* the matter with Robbie? What if his immune system had been weakened by now, like Martha's was? There must be a strong chance that Geraldine could lose him too. Mandy shut her eyes, trying to squeeze the thought out of her head. It was too painful to contemplate. Martha had become gravely ill so very quickly, and there had been nothing they could do to help her. Would the same thing happen to Robbie?

Nine

'Well, you were spot on about those rats,' said
Emily Hope, smiling at Mandy after they'd said
goodbye to a grateful Mr Marsh. 'I'm sure they'll
be right as rain once their litter's been changed.
Good diagnosis, love!'

'Thanks,' Mandy said, absent-mindedly fiddling
with a stray wood shaving that had fallen out of the
cage.

'And your teacher seems very nice,' her mum
went on, busily spraying the tabletop with disinfec-
tant. 'Are you getting on better with him now?'

'Um, yes. I suppose so,' Mandy replied, sticking
the tiny shred of wood into her pocket.

'So what is it, then?' her mother asked, throwing

the paper towel in the bin and washing her hands. 'What's on your mind? Spit it out, love. I can see something's bothering you.'

Mandy wasn't sure what to do. She felt as though putting her fears into words might make them come true, but she knew her mother would have something sensible to say. Besides, she wanted to hear her professional opinion. Mrs Hope leaned against the worktop, her hands in the pockets of her white coat, watching Mandy patiently.

'It's Robbie, Mum,' she confided at last. 'Do you think he's getting any better? Have you heard how he is from Geraldine? I know you couldn't find anything the matter with him, but surely he ought to be getting back to normal by now!'

'I agree,' her mother said. 'I've been worrying about him too – I spoke to Geraldine this morning when she came to collect Kitty. She says she's managed to get him to take a little of the liquid food I gave her, but he isn't very keen.' She sighed. 'When animals don't eat, it's a clear sign that something's wrong. I just can't work out what it is, though!'

'Do you think he's just pining for Martha?' Mandy asked.

'Could be,' her mother replied. 'They did have a very strong attachment, after all. The trouble is, he's getting quite old, and he needs to keep his strength up. If he carries on moping around like this and not eating properly, he'll get weaker and his body won't be able to cope with infection.'

Just like Martha, Mandy thought. 'Perhaps I shouldn't have suggested taking on the kitten to Geraldine,' she worried out loud. 'Maybe she won't be able to give Robbie all the time and attention he needs.'

'So you put that idea into her head, did you?' her mother smiled. 'I suspected as much. Oh, I should think Geraldine can cope. And if anything does happen to Robbie, she might be glad of another pet to help her get over it.'

'I hope you're right,' Mandy said, with a heavy heart. Despite her mother's reassurances, she was beginning to think that she might have done the wrong thing. If Robbie did end up suffering because of an idea she'd put in Geraldine's head, she'd never be able to forgive herself.

'Bye, Geraldine. Bye, you two,' Mrs Hope called, starting the Land-rover's engine after dropping Mandy and James off at Wood Vale the next day. 'Give me a ring this afternoon when you're ready to be picked up.'

Geraldine put an arm round their shoulders and took them inside the house. 'Come and see how

Kitty's getting on,' she said. 'I've got her on to the bottle now, and she loves it!'

'Have you still not decided what to call her?' James asked, grinning. 'If you're not careful, she'll stay Kitty for the rest of her life!'

'Well, that wouldn't be so bad,' Geraldine replied, as they went through to the kitchen. 'I've been tossing a couple of names around, but nothing seems quite right so far. Still, there's no rush. And here she is, in her new home!'

'Oh, she does look cosy,' Mandy said. The kitten was lying in a see-through plastic incubator on the counter top. She was being kept warm by a hot-water bottle, wrapped up in a towel and then covered again with a soft blue blanket.

'I started off with an infra-red lamp over the top of the incubator, but now she seems to prefer cud-dling up to the hot-water bottle,' Geraldine said. 'Isn't she adorable? It looks like one of her eyes is just beginning to open too. I could watch her for hours, even though she does seem to spend most of the time asleep!'

'And where's Robbie?' Mandy asked, glancing round the room. She'd been disappointed not to see him leaping up at Geraldine's heels when she answered the door, and his basket was empty.

Geraldine sighed. 'He's out in the garden,' she

said, pointing out of the window. 'I buried Martha in her favourite spot by the pond, and Robbie seems to know she's there. He spent all day yesterday sitting under the willow tree, as though he wants to be near her.'

'Poor thing,' Mandy murmured, standing beside Geraldine and watching the beagle. He lay at the foot of the tree with his head on his paws. From time to time he lifted his nose to sniff the air and gaze around, as though he was looking for someone. A light drizzle was falling, but he didn't seem to notice.

'You'd think he'd sooner stay in his basket on a day like this,' James said. 'He must be soaked through!'

'I'll go and bring him in in a minute,' Geraldine said. 'The trouble is, I know he'll just sit by the door and howl. I can't bear to hear him. He sounds so miserable!'

Suddenly Mandy remembered something. 'I thought you said he lay in his basket all the time?' she reminded Geraldine.

Geraldine sighed. 'He hasn't been near the basket for a couple of days,' she replied, fiddling with the end of a scarf tied round her neck. 'I'm afraid that could be my fault. I had to throw Mouse away, you see.'

'Mouse?' James asked, looking puzzled.

'The funny old stuffed toy Martha used to play with,' Geraldine explained, turning away from the window. 'Your mother told me to clean everything Martha had been in contact with. She said there was really no danger of Kitty catching FIV, but she might pick up something else. You know how vulnerable newborns are, especially if they haven't been passed any antibodies through their mother's milk. Mouse was falling to pieces – she wouldn't have survived the washing-machine. I thought it would be safer to get rid of her altogether.'

'And do you really think that's made such a difference to Robbie?' Mandy asked, concerned.

'It certainly looks like it,' Geraldine replied, pulling out a chair and sitting down at the kitchen table. 'I suppose Mouse smelled of Martha, and that comforted him. Now that there's nothing left in the basket to remind him of her, he doesn't want anything to do with it. He sat by the door the whole of last night. Whenever I came in to feed the kitten, there he was, in exactly the same position.'

'You must be tired,' James said. 'Tell us what we can do to help you out.'

'Shall we go and bring Robbie in?' Mandy added. 'Perhaps seeing some new faces might cheer him up.' She didn't really believe that, but she hated to see Geraldine looking so worried. There had to be something they could do to help!

'Thanks,' Geraldine said gratefully. 'I really need to feed the chickens now and collect up their eggs. If you two could bring Robbie in and try to feed him, that would be great. There's some special mince and egg I've cooked up in the fridge – he seems to have gone right off the liquid food.'

She looked at her watch and added, 'Kitty will need feeding again before too long, as well. You'll probably have more luck with her than Robbie!'

Mandy and James walked down the path towards the pond. On either side of them, the bushes dripped steadily. Raindrops misted Mandy's hair, and her trainers were soon soaked through. She shivered. It wasn't really cold, but the garden looked so dank and depressing. And there was Robbie, lying under the willow tree.

Mandy crouched down to pat his wet coat. 'Cheer up, boy,' she said encouragingly. 'Why don't you come back to the house with James and me?'

The beagle looked up at her with big, mournful eyes. He pushed his nose half-heartedly into her hand and then dropped it back down to rest on his paws again.

'Here, Robbie!' James called. 'I've found a stick for you. Go fetch!' He took a few steps away from the bank and hurled the stick in a graceful arc across the lawn. But Robbie just watched it land by the lavender hedge without bothering to make a move.

'Come on up to the house with us, Robbie,' Mandy repeated, stroking his ear. 'There's something delicious for you in the fridge!'

Together, they eventually persuaded the beagle to get to his feet and then they practically pushed him up the path to the back door of the cottage. Geraldine looked over from the chicken runs and gave them an encouraging wave.

'This must be his mince,' Mandy said, taking a plastic container out of the fridge once they were inside the kitchen. 'Perhaps we should heat it up a little, in case he doesn't like it so cold.'

Robbie sat by the door, watching them as they looked for a saucepan and then put his food on the stove to warm. When it was ready, James held Robbie's head steady while Mandy tried to spoon a little of the food into his mouth. It wasn't an easy job, though. If she did manage to get any morsels past Robbie's teeth, he spat them out again without swallowing.

'Oh, Robbie! Why are you being so stubborn!'

Mandy said at last in exasperation, sitting back on her heels. 'This is for your own good, you know. You've got to eat!'

'Let's stop for a while,' James suggested. 'We're not getting anywhere and, besides, I think Kitty's hungry. She's started to cry.'

Mandy looked over to the incubator. The kitten was lifting up her head and miaowing thinly as she struggled to move across the blanket in search of food. 'You're right,' Mandy said to James. 'After all, we might as well feed the one who actually wants us to.'

They got up from the floor. Immediately, Robbie went back over to sit by the door. He looked beseechingly up at them and whined to go out.

'You can stay here for the moment,' Mandy told him, fishing a feeding-bottle out of the steriliser. 'We're not giving up on you that quickly, you know.'

When they'd mixed up the kitten's milk, James took a turn feeding her. He held the little thing upright in the palm of his hand while she sucked greedily on the rubber teat of the bottle, her tiny paws wrapped round his fingers. 'She's really coming on,' he said, smiling at the kitten's eagerness to feed. 'Her fur is so soft!'

'Dad thinks she's a lilac Burmese,' Mandy said,

watching him enviously. 'That's a sort of pale lavender grey. She's going to be beautiful.'

When James had finished feeding the kitten,
Mandy took her from him and began to wipe her
with some damp cotton wool. 'You're going to have
a lovely time here when you've grown up some
more,' she told the young animal as she massaged
her tummy gently. 'There's a great big garden to
play in, and you've got Robbie here to keep you
company.'

She glanced towards the back door, and caught
sight of the beagle watching her intently. Hoping
to keep him interested, she carried on talking quietly to the kitten in the same encouraging tone of
voice. 'Yes, you and Robbie are going to be great
friends,' she said, nudging James's back at the
same time to get his attention.

'What's up?' he asked, turning round from the
sink where he'd been washing up the kitten's
bottle.

'Shh!' Mandy hissed. 'It's Robbie. Look at him!'

The beagle had begun padding hesitantly
towards her, his eyes fixed on the tiny creature she
was holding. 'This is Kitty,' Mandy told him,
crouching down on the floor so she was at Robbie's
level and offering him the kitten to examine.
'She's come to live here, with you and Geraldine.

Haven't you met her before?'

Robbie sniffed Kitty all over with his damp black nose. The little creature couldn't see or hear him, but managed to lift up her head towards the source of this strange new doggy smell. Robbie looked at Mandy inquiringly, as if he couldn't quite work out what was going on.

'Kitty's just a baby,' she said. 'Are you going to help us look after her?' She patted the beagle encouragingly with her other hand, still holding

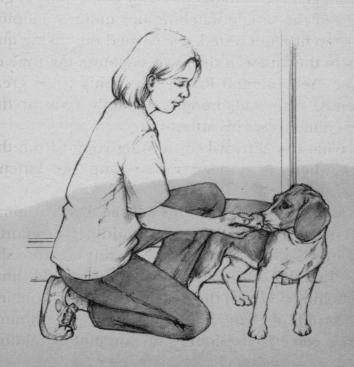

the kitten close to him.

Robbie stared down at the tiny animal. Then, very gently, he licked her head a couple of times with his clean pink tongue.

James let out his breath with a whoosh. Mandy gazed up at him, her eyes shining. 'I think Robbie's got the idea, don't you?' she said happily. 'Hang on! Where's he off to now?'

The beagle had turned away and was trotting purposefully across the room. When he'd reached his basket, he settled himself in it, looked over at Mandy and barked. He was asking for something, and she knew exactly what that something was.

'OK,' she smiled, walking over to the basket. 'Here you are.'

Carefully, she laid the kitten safely between his two front paws. Robbie bent his head and began to lick her steadily all over, just as he'd done with Martha in that very same place. Then he laid his head down beside her and closed his eyes. Anyone would have thought he was asleep, were it not for the steady thump, thump of his tail against the side of the basket.

'You don't think he might squash her, do you?' James asked Mandy quietly.

She shook her head, feeling too choked to speak, and tried to swallow the lump in her throat.

'He's not going to hurt a hair on her head,' she said eventually. 'And neither will anyone else, if he's around. Oh, let's go and fetch Geraldine, James. This is something she's got to see!'

Ten

This is the life! Mandy thought contentedly, putting her arms behind her head and closing her eyes as she lay back on the grass. The sun was warm on her face, and the scent of lavender blossom and freshly mown grass wafted over on the breeze. A blackbird was singing somewhere in the garden, and her parents were laughing as Geraldine recounted some long, complicated story about her Irish uncles.

It was the first weekend of the summer holidays, and Mandy, her parents and James had been invited over for lunch at Wood Vale. 'To thank you for all the help you've given me,' Geraldine had said. 'I couldn't have got through these past few weeks without you lot.'

'But I'm the one who should be thanking you!' Mandy had protested. 'I wouldn't have done half so well in biology if you hadn't helped me, Geraldine.'

Mr Marsh had given her top marks for the project, and he'd written her a great end-of-term report, too. It was funny how things could change, Mandy reflected, chewing on a blade of grass and remembering what she'd first thought of Mr Marsh. In the end, the whole class had been sorry to say goodbye to him – though of course it would be great to see Miss Temple again.

There was no need to think about school for the moment, though, Mandy decided. The long, glorious holidays lay ahead, and she was going to enjoy every second of them.

'Go fetch, Robbie!' she heard James calling, and there was the sound of something whistling through the air.

She propped herself up on her elbows to watch as the beagle raced after his ball, barking excitedly. He sniffed around the lavender bushes, ignoring a couple of bees who were busy among the flower spikes, before seizing the ball and carrying it triumphantly back to James. Wagging his tail happily, he dropped the ball at James's feet and stood with his head on one side, waiting expectantly for the next throw.

Suddenly, a small grey shape appeared from nowhere, streaking across the grass and pouncing on the ball. 'Angel!' Mandy laughed, jumping to her feet. 'What do you think you're doing? That's Robbie's toy – it's much too big for you!'

James rescued the ball and the kitten leaped away, skittering over the grass and shooting halfway up a tree trunk. Then she suddenly seemed to realise she'd climbed higher than she intended and looked down, miaowing piteously.

Mandy hurried over and gently unhooked the kitten's claws from the rough bark, holding her slender body tight. 'It's just as well you're so adorable,' she told the little cat sternly, feeling the beginnings of a purr vibrate in the soft fur beneath her fingers.

'And what kind of mischief is she up to now?' Geraldine asked, walking over towards them. 'I don't know whatever possessed me to call her Angel – we should have named her Trouble instead.' But there was a twinkle in her blue eyes.

'Angel is the perfect name for her, and you know it!' Mandy grinned, giving the kitten one last cuddle before setting her down on the ground. At once, she began to stalk a fly, waving her tail fiercely to and fro before she jumped up in the air – and then tumbled over her paws.

'You wouldn't have said so this morning,' Geraldine said, shaking her head solemnly. 'She'd climbed up on one of the kitchen chairs and was trying to catch poor Robbie's tail as he waved it back and forth. Then she decided it would be more fun to jump on his back and see if he'd take her for a ride!'

'And did he?' Mandy asked, laughing at the idea. Robbie was so patient and good-tempered, she could imagine him joining in with the game.

'Oh, she lost interest and fell off a second later,' Geraldine replied. She looked over to watch the beagle chasing his ball towards the orchard. 'Dear old Robbie never batted an eyelid! You should see the teasing he puts up with, and not so much as a bark out of him.'

'Angel seems to have given him a new lease of life, doesn't she?' Mandy commented.

Geraldine nodded. 'From the moment he started taking notice of her, he decided life was worth living after all.' She added, half smiling at the idea, 'It might sound crazy, but I sometimes think Martha's sent this kitten to look after him. That's really why I called her Angel.'

'I know just what you mean,' Mandy said, watching the little Burmese roll over on the grass. 'I was so sure she belonged here with you two. And she *is* beautiful, isn't she?'

Angel's coat had turned the softest shade of pinky grey, like a wisp of smoke, with darker points to her ears and nose. Her pale eyes, ringed with black, were particularly striking. It was impossible to pin down what colour they were – one minute golden, and then the next as clear as a shining pool of water.

'We ought to show those horrible Brewers how lovely she is,' Geraldine agreed, picking up the mischievous kitten and kissing the top of her head. 'They'd probably try to take her back, though, and we couldn't have that.'

James came over to join them with Robbie at his heels. 'Could I have another drink, please, Geraldine?' he asked, wiping his flushed face. 'This is thirsty work!'

'Of course,' she replied. 'There's more lemon-ade on the kitchen table, if you don't mind helping yourself. And if you're going that way, perhaps you could bring down some ice cream from the freezer? The bowls and spoons are out here already.'

'Sure,' James said, already starting on his way.

'I think Robbie could do with a drink too,' Mandy added, noticing how heavily the beagle was panting. 'Why don't we take him up with us?'

They walked back up to the cottage. Robbie followed them, Angel zigzagging around him as she darted from one side of the path to the other. Mandy knew that she'd only just had her final vaccinations, so she wasn't used to being outside. Everything fascinated her, from a dragonfly darting across the grass to a fat worm wriggling through the soil. The garden must have seemed like one big playground.

'Come on, Angel, in you go,' Mandy said, scooping the kitten up and carrying her through the back door. 'I bet you'd like a drink as well.'

As soon as they were inside the cool kitchen, she put Angel down by her saucer of water. Robbie made straight for his own bowl and began to lap noisily. When he'd had a good long drink, he padded over to his basket and settled down comfortably.

'Looks like I've managed to tire him out,' James smiled, draining his glass of lemonade.

Mandy looked round from the freezer with two tubs of ice cream in her hands. 'Robbie's not the only one,' she said, nodding her head in Angel's direction. After a more dainty drink, the kitten was now following Robbie over to the basket. With one big leap, she jumped inside, stepped delicately over the beagle's legs and curled herself up between his front paws and his chin. In a couple of seconds, both animals were fast asleep.

'I think Martha would approve, don't you?' James said quietly.

'Definitely!' Mandy said, smiling down at the pair of them. Then, with a happy sigh, she turned towards the door. 'Let's go, James,' she said. 'If we stand here much longer, my hands will freeze and this ice cream will melt!'

And, together, they went happily back out into the sunshine.